BEGIN AGAIN

TAYLOR EPPERSON

For Griffin.
For loving me in my mess, always.
I love you.

This one is also for the survivors, you are so strong. And for all the people who believed us when we came forward, thank you thank you thank you.

June 2024 - Annie is 28, Sam is 30

It's been one hundred and sixty-two days since I last saw my husband. As I move away from the window that faces the ocean at the resort I'm staying at, I frown down at my phone. I'm in Hawaii for the first time and all I can think about is how long it's been since I last saw Sam.

"Get a grip," I whisper to myself and put my phone back up to my ear. "I'm still here."

My brother, Noah, called to drop the bomb that because his flight was canceled, he's going to need me and Sam to confirm everything is good to go for his wedding.

"Good. And you'll be okay helping Sam out and making sure everything is good for me and Tally?" he asks again, since I didn't actually give him an answer when he asked me a few seconds ago.

"Not a problem," I tell my brother the words he wants to hear, the words that I would love to believe. But as I sit on the soft comforter that covers the huge king-sized bed, I wish the words were true. I lie back on the soft blankets and wonder if the bed will swallow me whole so I don't have to talk to anyone.

My older brother and his fiancé decided to have a destination wedding in Maui. I've already arrived, but my brother, his fiancé, and her family are all stuck in Utah for an extra twenty-four hours because of their canceled flight. Not a problem. Except the fact that I'm about to see my husband for the first time in six months. Sam is my brother's best friend and the best man. He's also my husband, which no one but the two of us and my closest friends knows about.

Then my brother drops another bomb on me. "He will have to stay in your room. I already called the resort and they said he won't be able to check in because our room is under my name, not his."

I sit up so quickly my head spins. I squeeze my eyes shut. "But you explained the situation?" My voice isn't frantic, but everything is different now. Though Sam and I have slept together in the same room—even in the same bed—sharing a space with him after so long apart might be awkward. Especially with how I left things.

"I did." Noah's voice dips low like it always does when he feels bad. "Sorry, Sis, they have weird rules and only I can check in."

I close my eyes and try to take my mind to one of those meditations that my therapist told me to try. I imagine a woman with a British accent telling me to imagine my favorite place in the world. My husband's beautiful tanned face appears in my mind and my eyes fly open.

Meditation does not work.

"That's fine," I say. Maybe Sam will sleep on the floor. Wait, no. I'd never make him sleep on the floor. Not with his bad back. I wipe a sweaty palm on the comforter beside me.

"Will you text him your room info?" Noah is asking, but I'm

not really listening. What can I do in the next half hour to be ready to see Sam? I've planned our reunion several times in my head, and none of my scenarios included sharing a hotel room.

"I will," I say. While it's not ideal, I'm grateful that I flew in yesterday. I've never been to Hawaii and wanted a day to myself before the chaos of the wedding party descended upon the resort. But I expected Noah and Tally to be here as a buffer between me and Sam. Now my buffer is gone.

"Alright," Noah says, and I glance around the room that seemed so big a minute ago. "Thanks, Sis."

"Mhm," I murmur before hanging up.

I scroll on my phone and start playing "Welcome To New York." Taylor's Version of course. Taylor is probably the only person in the world who will be able to calm my nerves right now, and 1989 is my favorite album. The familiar notes fill the room and my heart rate slows.

Then I scroll to my texts. There's already one from Sam waiting for me.

SAM HOLLAND

Noah said he was going to call you. I'm about five minutes out from the resort. What's your room number?

My gut clenches. I hate how civil he's being. I wish he would fight or scream or yell or ask me where I've been for the last six months. And a deeper wish—a desire really—I have is that he'll show up and wrap me up in his arms and tell me just how much he's always loved me and everything between us will be easy and normal like it was before. But I'm not holding out hope for that. I'm not even sure I'm ready for that.

I scroll up in our text thread, the last text from him—that I left on read—was from the day after I left.

I never answered and he isn't the pushy type, something I'm usually thankful for. But right now, I wish that I had tried a little bit harder to close the space between us. He might have left the ball in my court, but I still wish he would have tried. But maybe he didn't reach out for all the same reasons I didn't. I wanted to, but the thought of my heart breaking again because of him stopped me.

Nothing will be able to save my broken heart now. I text him the room number and try to focus on the music while I wait.

The final notes of "Out of the Woods" fade when the doorbell rings. Because of course, my brother would want to get married at a resort where the rooms have doorbells. I don't think I've ever stayed in a place so fancy, not that I've traveled much.

I pull myself up to a standing position and slowly walk to the door, taking a deep breath as I grab the handle. I can do this.

I open the door and I swear I go weak at the knees. I clutch the doorknob like it's my lifeline. Sam's light blue eyes meet mine—searching my face—and my body goes warm. He grins at me, the smile that has always been just mine.

"Hey, sunshine," he says and my entire body turns into complete jelly. "Can I come in?"

Not trusting my voice, I simply pull the door open wider and let my husband into the room.

PART ONE

1

ANNIE

August 2010 - Annie is 14, Sam is 16

"I know that look." My best friend Emily sits down in the chair across from me at the small table I've been reading at while she peruses the library shelves for the book she needs to read for English. School starts next week and she hasn't done any of the reading yet.

"What look?" I slide my bookmark into my well-worn copy of *Emma* and look at her.

"The look that says you're mad at your mom again and you're trying to forget about how awful she is by reading *Emma*. Again."

I frown.

"See. I know I'm right." Emily drops the heavy classic, *Huckleberry Finn,* on the table.

"Is that the large print edition?" I ask. Better to talk about books than to think about the fight I had with Mom this morning. I'd pretty much rather do anything than think about Mom. I'm only fourteen and I'm already daydreaming about the day when I can go to college or at least move out. Too bad I don't know what I like yet, other than books. But I don't know if you can study books in college.

She nods. "The only copy they have left."

"I read it in June." I'm not trying to be smug about it, but she really shouldn't have waited this long.

Emily rolls her eyes. "Of course you did. You are the nerd in this friendship."

I smile, secretly pleased, though I'd never dare call myself a nerd. The popular girls don't need me to give myself a nickname. The kids at school already call me Freckles because of all the freckles that cover my skin—which isn't exactly all that original, but it's better than being dubbed the class nerd. "I prefer the term bookworm, but I'll take it I guess."

Emily's laugh echoes through the quiet library. I glance around but no one is paying attention to us. She stares at the thick book in front of her. "Is this book even any good?"

"I am the wrong person to ask." She knows I have a fondness for classic books, so of course I thought it was good. I fell in love with old books back before Dad left our family and Mom used to read to me and Noah every night. I visit Narnia at least once a year and I'm a huge fan of Anne Shirley, after all, she's kind of my namesake.

"Can you believe we start school next week?" She changes the subject again and pulls me away from thoughts of all the books I love and brings me to my second love, school. "And we'll officially be freshmen!"

"I am excited for school." I twist my hands in my lap, not saying anything else. Emily knows that I've been fighting with Mom all summer. Mom got a new boyfriend and he's been stinking up the house because all he does is smoke, drink beer, and watch our TV. Mom told me I needed to be nicer to Jeff, but he's a lazy jerk, so why should I have to be nice? At least he's better than her last boyfriend, if that's even possible.

So yeah, I'm excited about school starting because it means I can spend most of my time away from home and I'll have homework to do when I am there. Plus, I love learning. Emily on the other hand is excited for completely different reasons.

"Do you think there will be any cute boys this year?" She gets that dreamy look in her eyes, the one she always gets when she's thinking about her latest crush or the opportunity she'll have next week to have a new crush.

I scrunch my nose. "There's more to life than boys."

"There's more to life than books," she retorts.

We're sitting at a table right by the library entrance and before I can say something back to Emily, a guy walks into the library and I watch as Emily sits up a little straighter while I lean back in my chair trying to be invisible. But I can't pry my eyes away from him as he walks into the library.

We live in a small town and I've never seen him before. He's got dark brown hair and he's wearing a faded gray T-shirt. His jaw isn't sharp, like jaws are often described in books, but he looks almost as if he's still got a baby face. At least, he looks a little boyish and I'll be the first to admit that this guy is attractive. In a best friend sort of way. But that's all I'll ever admit.

I've seen Mom date so many stupid men and get hurt and screwed over by them that I already know I never want a boyfriend or a husband. Emily on the other hand? She's probably fantasizing already about how many kids she and this guy will have once they get married in seven years.

The guy glances over to our table and our eyes meet. He's younger than I realized, probably my age or Noah's age. Even with the ten or so feet between us, I can already tell he has the bluest eyes of anyone I've ever seen. I give him a friendly, but embarrassed smile and then look back to Emily who's already waving the boy over, because of course she is. She didn't even last ten seconds before wanting to introduce herself to him. I hold back an eye-roll.

"Hi!" She gives him her biggest grin. Emily is pretty, like insanely pretty. She's got long wavy auburn hair and stunning brown eyes. She's also got a smile that could make any person fall in love with her, I'm sure of it. And because we live in a small town of farmers, she's always stood out. I mean, I stand out too, with my fiery red hair and all, but not like she does.

"Hey," the guy says, shoving his hands deep into the front pockets of his pants. His arms are tan, like he's spent most of the summer in the sun. I wonder where he's from.

"I'm Emily, and this is Annie," she says, gesturing between the two of us and somehow quenches my desire to actually know more about him. She can do all the talking. They'll be dating by the end of the first week of school. Whereas I can't seem to form a normal sentence around a boy I think is cute up to this point in my life so I offer him another small wave and hope he leaves our table soon.

"I'm Sam. Could either of you tell me where to go to get a library card?"

I see Emily's shoulders droop. He likes books, so not her go-to man. She likes the jocks who like to tell her she's pretty. She had her first real kiss last year, something that I've only read about in books and I am more than okay with that.

"I've got to run," she tells Sam. "But Annie loves the library, so I'm sure she can help you."

I blink in surprise and try to get her attention without being obvious about it. I can't be left with this guy on my own, but she refuses to look at me, as if she knows I'll try to stop whatever her plan is. I snap my fingers in her direction, but they both ignore me while she grins up at him.

Emily holds up her huge copy of *Huckleberry Finn*. "I've

got to read this before school next week, and it's going to take all of my time." Then she finally looks at me. "Text me later?"

"Okay," I say as I try not to glare at her, but I want to.

Emily grabs her bag and heads out the door to head home and I'm alone with Sam. "The main desk is just down the hall," I say pointing. "They should be able to get you a library card."

He nods and looks down at the table where *Emma* is lying and I squirm in my seat the longer he stares.

He finally breaks the silence. "Is that one any good?"

"It's my favorite," I say.

He nods like this is what he expected me to say. Though, most girls our age are very into *Twilight* right now, so I'm pretty sure a classic being my favorite isn't at all what he expected me to say.

"I'll have to read it sometime." He gives me a smile, one that makes the edges of his eyes crinkle.

My heart does a funny little flip. "Let me know if you need to borrow a copy." I blurt before I remember that we are in a library, where he could get his own copy. "I mean, if you want. I've got another copy." More like five, but he doesn't need to know that. Most people already think I'm the weirdo who likes classic books.

My whole body feels warm. This is why I don't talk to boys. I get all hot and sweaty and blurt out stupid things.

His smile only grows as if he hasn't even noticed my embarrassment, and with that look it feels like a ray of sunshine straight to my chest. I look down at my hands again. Is this what Mom and Emily feel when guys smile at them? Is that why they keep choosing to date guys who are losers because of how their smiles send a physical jolt into their bodies?

"I'd like that. I'm new to town, so it'd be nice to have a friend," he says, his voice soft and quiet.

I didn't know it was possible, but I feel myself grow even

warmer and I know that my skin is bright red. I can't look at him, not with this reaction.

"Where did you move from?" I mumble without looking up.

"Texas, but before that it was New York, upstate, and Washington before that."

"Wow." I'm startled by his history. "I've never even left Colorado."

He looks at me like he's about to let me in on some sort of secret. "Guess you'll have to change that sometime." He glances down the hall toward the reception desk. "I'd better get my library card, but I'll see you around?"

"Sure," I say, but I don't mean it. I'm not like Emily. I don't flirt with guys or get their numbers to hang out with them. I spend most of my time either at home or at the library or at school.

"Good," he says as if that settles the matter as if we're already friends. "See you."

I offer another small wave—one of the only things I seem to be capable of today—as he walks away. His butt looks good in his jeans. I scramble up out of my seat at the thought, grabbing my copy of *Emma* and stuffing it into my bag. I can't look at his butt, that's weird, right?

Emily would have no trouble staring at him as he walked away, but I'm not her. Boys don't notice me and I don't want them to. But when I glance up at Sam again, he's looking at me while he waits for the librarian to finish talking on the phone.

This time, he's the one who waves. Butterflies swirl in my stomach as I leave in a rush.

2

———

SAM

August 2010 - Sam is 16, Annie is 14

"I've already picked your partners for the project, there will be no switching." My English teacher, Ms. Clements announces that our first assignment this semester will be a group project. A group of two people. It's only the first week of school and I'm still the new kid. Most kids in my class are not excited about the assignment, but this could be a good way for me to meet someone in my grade. I met Annie and Emily last week at the library, but I haven't seen them since.

I haven't been able to get Annie out of my head. Her bright red hair and shy smile makes me smile just thinking about it. I've been looking out for her here at school, but I haven't seen her around yet.

"Raise your hands when your name is called, since I know we have some new faces," Ms. Clements says as she starts to read out the list of names. I listen carefully for my name. "Sam Holland," I raise my hand, "you'll be with Noah Jones."

I scan the room and see a scrawny kid with dark blonde hair raising his hand. He gives me a nod and I offer a friendly wave.

After Ms. Clements announces all of the groups, we're given time to meet up with our partner to discuss which Greek myth we want to use for our project. I make my way over to Noah, sitting in the seat in front of his desk. "I'm Sam, I just moved here."

Noah runs a hand through his hair. "Cool. I'm Noah. I have to work most days after school, but I'm free in the evenings and during lunch hour."

"That works for me."

I don't have a job yet. I'm only a junior and my parents haven't made me get a job since we just moved here. They want me to make friends here first, which would be fine if I knew we'd be here longer than a year. I don't like getting attached to people because we move so often, because Dad gets antsy and likes to regularly change up what he does for work. My younger sister, Amelia, and I already have bets that Dad won't last one year as a cow farmer. She thinks he'll last a month longer than I do. Our other younger sister, Jodi, isn't old enough to know that this will be a pattern throughout her life.

When you move around so often, it's hard to make any real friends. I'm good at the surface level, but I don't let myself get attached because it's too hard when you have to say goodbye.

Before we decide what myth we'll be using for our project, the bell rings. Noah hands me a piece of paper. "That's my address. I don't have a car, so I hope you do."

I let out a laugh as I look at the paper in my hand. "You won't need a car to get to my house. I live next door."

☀

As I approach Noah's house the next afternoon, loud voices are coming from inside the house. I give a heavy knock. Noah opens the door a second later, his hair is slightly rumpled as if he just woke up from a nap, and the yelling I heard before gets louder.

"We can work in my room," Noah says, gesturing for me to come in. There's a woman standing in the doorway of the kitchen who I assume is Noah's mother, she's yelling at a tall man who's slouching on the couch and his eyes are closed, I'm not even sure he's awake. Though I'm not sure how anyone could sleep with someone yelling at them like that.

"Sounds good." I follow Noah down the hallway. We walk past a room with an open door where I stop in my tracks and blink into the small, bright room. On the bed reading *Emma* is Annie, the girl I met at the library. She doesn't look up from her book.

My heart stutters.

It's her. Annie. She's been next door this whole time.

"That's just my younger sister," Noah says and when I look over at him, he's watching me.

Thankfully, he doesn't seem to notice that my heart has started to beat faster than normal. "She likes to read a lot. And hide away from my mom when she's yelling like this, not that I blame her."

It's impossible to ignore the profanity coming from the front room. Though, I'm trying.

"Cool," I nod. I don't tell him that I already met her, and I don't say that I've been wondering what she's been up to for the past week because I don't want to sound like a weirdo. I don't tell him that I also like to read. Seeing her again though is like a bright light in the darkness of a new place. *She's familiar, that's all.* That's what I tell myself as we enter his small bedroom and he quietly shuts the door.

"Sorry about my mom, she's been yelling at this boyfriend for days and he hasn't left yet. It's annoying, but I'd rather her yell at the men she dates than yell at Annie about something."

"She yells at your sister?" I ask. I have two younger sisters and even though they can be annoying, my mom has never yelled at them the way Noah's mom is yelling right now. I feel like I need to clean out my ears.

Noah nods, slowly. "Far too often. I have to calm Mom down after. Annie is good at standing up to her, but it's annoying. Mom always thinks she's right though, so I feel like I can't do too much. Anyway, let's work on the project and not talk about my family's issues."

I try to focus on our project, but my mind wanders to Annie, in the room next door, and I wonder how she feels about all the yelling. If I ever get the chance, I'll try to talk to her about it, make sure she knows that parents aren't supposed to yell like that at other people, much less their children.

3

ANNIE

October 2010 - Annie is 14 Sam is 16

I sort of have the house all to myself tonight. Mom's out at a party and Noah is at work, but it's Halloween, so the doorbell keeps ringing.

I throw my book onto the couch, wishing more than ever that I could just enjoy a quiet, relaxing evening, but I don't think that's going to happen. When I open the door, I see the entire Holland family gathered. The two girls—Sam's younger sisters—hold up their pumpkin buckets. "Trick-or-treat," they say together.

Against Mom's wishes, I put a handful of chocolate bars into each of their buckets. Mom's not here, so she won't know how much candy I'm giving away.

"You're the cutest little Dorothy," I say to his youngest sister, Jodi. I've only seen her a few times because mostly I stick to myself, but she seems nice and cute with her two missing front teeth.

"Thanks." She gives me a big toothless smile. "I love my red ruby slippers! They sparkle." She sticks out a foot to show me.

"Do you know who I am?" Amelia huffs. She's wearing all white and has two buns on either side of her head.

"Princess Leia of course," I say. My knowledge of *Star Wars* is fairly limited, but I have seen the movies once and I know who she is. Amelia grins.

Sam is watching me interact with his sisters. I've felt his gaze on me the entire time, and I finally let myself look at him. The same butterflies I felt back when we first met a couple months ago swirl in my belly. I don't know if I'll ever be able to squish these weird feelings I have. "And you must be Clark Kent."

He grins at me and pushes the glasses he's wearing—the ones with no lenses—up his nose. "How'd you guess?"

"The glasses, the button-up shirt that's slightly opened revealing your Spiderman shirt," I say.

Their mom chuckles.

"Superman, but close enough," he says. I feel myself go warm all over. Superheroes aren't my thing. "You stuck here handing out candy?"

I nod.

His mom frowns and his dad is already walking down the path with the two girls to go to the next house. "You shouldn't be alone on a night like tonight," she says. "You should come with us. Leave the bowl of candy out like we did, and come trick or treating."

I can't remember the last time I went trick-or-treating. Mom has almost always had some sort of party with her friends on Halloween, so Noah and I were left to our own devices. And usually, for me, that meant curling up with a good book. I could get candy when I wanted it, but a night reading without Mom's interruptions? That didn't happen very often these days.

"Um."

"Come on," Mrs. Holland says, smiling encouragingly at me. "It'll be fun."

I glance at Sam. He and I have hung out a couple of times, and by hung out I mean that I was in the room doing homework or something while he and Noah hung out. And it's not like we'll be alone, but maybe I can get to know him better. "Sure."

I grab my jacket and dump the rest of the candy bag into the bowl. I set it on our front porch and lock the front door.

"How long have you lived in Kersey?" she asks as we walk to the next house to catch up with the rest of Sam's family.

"My whole life," I answer.

"I grew up in the same place too, a little town in Vermont," she says. "But we move around a lot now."

Sam laughs. "That's one way to put it." He falls into step with me when we reach his family and his mom moves to be with her husband. "I don't think we've stayed in one place for more than a year my entire life."

"Oh yeah?" I look up at him. He's not too much taller than me, maybe five inches or so, but I still have to look up to meet his eyes.

"Yup." He stuffs his hands into the pockets of his jacket. "Dad's a bit of a dreamer. And he gets bored easily so we're always hopping around from place to place so he can try new jobs."

"Oh." I'm not really sure what to say to that. My dad also got bored. So bored that he left us when I was younger. I don't think about him much, because I don't really remember him. But my mom grew up here. "Mom doesn't ever want to leave here."

"Yeah, that's what Noah told me. Do you want to leave here?" he asks.

I shift uncomfortably. "I don't know. Kersey is home, you know?" And even with all the fights I have with Mom, I can't really see myself going anywhere else. I've never even left the state of Colorado. The world is huge and intimidating.

"I don't." Sam grins at me. "I've never stayed in a place long enough for anywhere to feel like home."

"That's kind of sad," I say. I can't imagine not having roots somewhere. I feel like it would be awful to not know how long you were going to stay somewhere.

"They just gave me a king-size Twix," Jodi yells with glee as we cross over to the next street. I smile and while I miss my book, I'm glad I decided to come.

"Dad is a dreamer," Sam says, making me look back up at him. His jaw is tight. "His latest dream that brought us here is to be a cow farmer. Does the man know anything about cows or farming? Not until we moved here a couple of months ago."

I laugh. A full belly laugh.

"You think that's funny?"

"I think it must be nice to be able to pick up your life and do whatever you want." The truth of the words hit me as I say them. I'm only fourteen, but I wonder what I want to do with my life. Maybe there is a future for me outside of this small town.

"It might be, if you weren't the one who had to keep starting over," Sam grumbles quietly so his parents don't hear him.

I resist the urge I have to reach out and touch him. To offer him some sort of comfort. But this is the first time we've really had any sort of conversation, so touching would probably be weird. "I bet it's hard, moving so much."

"I'd love to have a place to call home, you know?" His eyes twinkle under the streetlight we're standing under. "I can't ever get too attached to a place or to people. It makes it hard to make friends."

"You and Noah seem to be good friends."

Sam shrugs. "Noah's easy to get along with."

"I hope that we can be friends, too." I have to glance away after the words come out. I'm never this forward with anyone except maybe Emily. But there's something about Sam that makes me want to be around him, to be his friend. Sure, he's cute. But that doesn't have anything to do with it. I want to be his friend because something about him makes me want to be close to him.

"I'd like that."

When I look up at him again, he's smiling. So I smile back. "Friends then."

"Friends."

We fall into an awkward silence. "I should warn you, I don't know how to be friends with a boy. Emily is my only friend, besides Noah,

, but I don't think he counts because he's my brother."

"Well, then I guess now's a good time to tell you that I don't really have friends that are girls. Most girls tend to look at me like I'm some sort of new plaything because I'm always the new kid."

"That's dumb." I roll my eyes. "There's more to life than romance and kissing and all that stuff. Because we can be friends without all that stuff. Kissing I mean. We don't need to kiss."

Shut your mouth, stop talking about kissing. Why are you even thinking about kissing? Maybe because Emily was just telling me about her new crush and how kissable his lips are. Gross. I don't need to be kissing anyone. Especially not Sam. He does have nice lips though.

Gah. Stop it.

I force myself to look at Sam. He's watching me with a bemused expression on his face.

"I haven't ever thought about kissing you," I blurt. Until now. Now I wonder what it would be like to kiss him—or anyone really. "Sorry, I'm making this awkward. Can we stop talking about kissing?"

He smirks. "I think you're the only one talking about kissing. But yes, we can stop."

"Thank you," I breathe in relief. "Friends still? Even though I blurt out awkward things?"

"I like it." He gives me a shy smile. "Makes me feel less awkward for the moment when I'll blurt out something awkward. Cause I'm sure it will happen. This is new territory for me. Making real friends."

I smile back. "Well, we can be awkward friends together, I guess."

"Perfect."

And just like that, I have my first boy friend.

4

———

SAM

January 2011 - Sam is 16 Annie is now 15

January in Colorado is bitter cold. I never thought I'd be colder than when I lived in upstate New York, but by the way the hairs inside my nose are freezing, I think I am wrong.

"Hurry up, man." I pull my coat closer around me and look down the dark street, but it doesn't fully block out the wind chill.

"Could you be quiet?" Noah, my best friend, whispers as we sneak along the side of a house. We just drove fifteen minutes into Greeley so that he could ask out a girl for prom—which is four months away. This whole thing is ridiculous.

"Well, maybe if you would hurry," I say, my breath fogging up in front of me. I was enjoying reading a book in my warm bed when Noah showed up at my door, and when he wants to go out, you say yes. Because getting him to get out of the house seems nearly impossible. I thought I was a homebody, but it turns out the Jones' siblings are even more so than I am.

I like to get out and go on adventures, at least most of the time. But when the temperature is in the negatives, I really don't want to leave the house. That's when I want to be home with my family or curled up with a book.

"Don't be such a grump," he snaps, the poster in his hand blowing in the wind.

"Why are we doing this again?" I'm fairly certain my nose will fall off if he doesn't hurry. Because of course, we couldn't have parked in front of Lacey's house. He made me park a street over and walk to her house so she didn't see his car.

"Because she'll get asked by some dude at her school if I don't ask her now," Noah tells me.

Kersey—where we live—has a small high school, so prom is combined with one of the Greeley high schools. Noah's had a crush on Lacey for who knows how long and she's finally single so now is his chance. At least, that's what he told me when he asked if I could give him a ride into town. Out of the two of us, I'm the only one with a car and there's no way his mom would have let him borrow hers for this. Which I find a tiny bit hypocritical because she wants Annie to be boy obsessed so she can find a husband—Annie is only fourteen—and thinks that Noah is wasting his time dating and should be making money instead.

Finally, we reach Lacey's front porch where Noah sets up the poster and the candy before ringing the bell. I'm a popsicle as I watch him turn before he takes off.

"Come on man," he yells as he sprints away from her house.

It is too cold to move that fast. I see the light spill onto the grass as someone opens the front door. I swerve into the neighbor's yard and I hear a woman call for Lacey as I crouch down behind a bush so she doesn't see me. Is this what it's like to have actual friends? You hide in the bushes when they leave you in the dust so his future prom date doesn't catch you?

I try not to get too attached to places or people. I know we won't be here long enough for it to matter.

But there's something about the Jones siblings that makes it hard to stay away. He is my best friend, but she is right up there in the mix. When I'm with her we talk about books and I like the fact that she looks at me like I'm an actual person, not someone who's just around to make out with. I'm always the new, shiny, cute guy that girls don't actually want to get to know. I've moved around enough that I know not to make friends with most girls, especially the popular ones. But with Annie, it's always been easy.

Maybe someday she will look at me like she wants to kiss me. The thought comes out of nowhere and I fall on my butt into frozen, icy snow.

"Crap," I whisper and stand, brushing off my backside. Lacey's front door is closed now, so I head in the direction of my parked truck.

I catch up to Noah and push the thought of kissing Annie out of my head. We've talked about this, we're friends. And friends do not kiss. It would be in my best interest to lock the thought about kissing her away before it bubbles into something more.

Noah grins at me as we get into my truck. His grin is so much like Annie's that my mind goes straight to her, and I bite my cheek to keep from smiling. Yesterday, she and I talked after school. I don't think it's because she likes me, but because she didn't want to go inside her house. Noah was working though, so it was just the two of us. I kept looking at her lips while she talked, and her eyes because you could see she was genuinely happy to be talking to me. But I don't think that friends look at their friend's lips when they're talking.

Before I turn on my truck, I close my eyes and lose myself in a daydream for half a second while Noah rambles about how awesome prom is going to be.

I can almost feel Annie in my arms, what it would be like to press my lips against hers.

"We gonna head home?" Noah asks, snapping me back to reality.

"Yup." I turn the key in the ignition and swallow thickly. Annie is different than the other people I've dated in the past. She's quiet, and bookish, and makes everything in my life a bit brighter. I always look forward to seeing her. My thoughts are lost in her as I drive back to Kersey.

"Is there someone you think you'll ask?" Noah interrupts my thoughts as we turn onto our street. I shake myself, I can't start crushing on Annie. I don't do anything serious. I've kissed girls in the past, and have gone on a few dates. But I can't do a crush. It feels too serious to let myself actually fall for someone.

"I don't think so," I say. I haven't found any girls other than Annie particularly interesting and I don't think Noah would like it if I asked her out. Knowing him, he'd probably make me promise not to ever date her because he's just that type of brother. The one who doesn't want to see her get hurt. And I won't be here in Colorado long, so the chances of me hurting her are pretty high. I can't like her.

I'm not in one place long enough to date someone seriously, which is why I haven't. I might only be sixteen, but some part of me craves putting down some roots already. I know better than to tell Mom and Dad that we should live somewhere longer than a year at most, because my words will just fall on deaf ears. I can't wait to settle down someday though.

"You should find someone, and we could go together," he says as I pull into my driveway. The lights from my house are glowing onto the front yard, but Noah's house looks dark. Annie must not be home. "Want to come over for a bit? We could watch a movie or see if Annie wants to play a card game, she's probably reading or something in her room."

"Sure," I reply, biting my lip to distract my thoughts about Annie, because now that I've wondered what it would be like to kiss her, I can't seem to get that image out of my head. I have to stop thinking about her though because she's my best friend's sister and could be one of my best friends if I keep my feelings out of the way. I won't ruin any sort of lasting friendship I have with her for a crush. I can be her friend. "And I'll think about the dance."

Noah grins at me. "You'll come around."

The week's old snow crunches under our feet as we walk to Noah's house. He unlocks the door and as it swings open, angry voices greet us from the kitchen. Apparently, everyone is home.

"If you'd stop eating so many cookies, maybe a guy would notice you."

My gut clenches at the way Annie's mom speaks to her and Noah freezes in front of me.

"Seriously, Mom, do you even hear yourself?" Annie yells back. "An extra cookie here and there is not the reason why guys don't notice me. And I'm only fourteen, shouldn't I not be worried about guys right now?"

Annie's mom huffs. "With that attitude, you'll never get married. Men like skinny women."

I swallow the bile in my throat. The first time I heard Annie's mom talk about things like this, I was shocked. My mom would never say something like that to either one of my younger sisters or any other person in general. I clench my fist. Why would someone talk to their daughter this way? The daughter could probably gain a few pounds if anyone is being honest. Annie eats like a bird, and I'm afraid she'll get snapped like a twig if she's not careful.

"I'm fourteen," Annie yells back.

"All the more reason to think about your future. You spend too much of your time with your nose stuck in books."

"Can you even hear yourself, Mom?" Annie asks again, her voice a little quieter now, but I can still hear the bitterness there.

"And I'm not even eating cookies, I'm making spaghetti. You sound delusional!"

"Don't you dare talk to me that way," their mom yells and then she storms out the backdoor.

"I'm gonna go see if I can talk to her," Noah says—talking about his mom. He's always trying to fix things, but I don't think anything will fix this. His mom needs a reality check. "Could you check on Annie?"

"Sure," I say and head toward the kitchen. I find her at the stove, cooking some pasta.

"Hi," I say as I approach her.

"Hi." She doesn't look at me, and anger oozes off of her.

"You okay?" I step closer so we're only a foot or so apart. I ignore the way my traitorous heart beats faster at her proximity. So much for getting rid of this crush. If anything, it's going to grow the more I hang out with her, not that I want to stop.

She sighs and even though she's angry, there's warmth in her eyes when she looks up at me. "All of that started because I told her I was going to make us some spaghetti for dinner after she told me she didn't have a plan because she figured you and Noah would get some food. The woman would rather me starve than eat something."

I look up at the ceiling as I lean against the counter. "Spaghetti is always a good choice."

"Thank you." She glances back at the pot of boiling water. "This might be horrible to say, but I can't wait until I'm old enough to move out."

It's not funny, but I let out a laugh. "I don't blame you. Where will you go?"

She stirs the marinara sauce as it starts to bubble. "New York maybe. They have a good culinary school I think. And I like food." She glances toward the side door that Noah and her mom went out of. "Too much, according to my mother. But I started cooking more this school year after my cooking class last semester, and I like it."

"Don't listen to her," I say, wishing I could do more to help her and tell her mom to shut up. But that's not my place. We're friends, but I don't know if that would be crossing some sort of boundary. "And you should go to a culinary school if that's what you want."

She sighs like she wishes it could be that easy and looks up at me. "Did Noah ask Lacey to prom?"

I nod. Changing the subject I see. "Yup, and I nearly lost my nose."

She laughs. "It's really cold this winter."

"Which is why spaghetti is a great dinner." My stomach rumbles as I tell her this.

She frowns. "I wish I could spend more dinners at your house. At least your mom likes me and doesn't comment on my eating habits."

I smile down at her, looking over all the freckles that cover her face. "You know you're welcome over there anytime."

"Yeah well, maybe once Mom gets a new job I'll come over more. She'll get mad if I'm not here for dinner. Which doesn't make any sense, but I feel like it's been a long time since anything she did made any sense."

I nod. Right now, at sixteen, Noah is paying for their rent on the house because their mom hasn't found a new job. She hasn't had a job in five of the six months that my family has lived here. At least she broke up with her boyfriend right before Christmas, but now there's a new guy hanging around the Jones' house all the time which Noah informed me is the norm for his mom. She goes through boyfriends like changing your clothes through the seasons. I've also noticed that she's grouchy nearly all the time. Between working almost thirty hours a week and going to school, it's a wonder that Noah is as happy as he is. Amazingly, Annie is warm and kind, unlike their mother.

"Can't wait," I say and Annie leans over and gives me a half hug. I stiffen, my heart beats erratically in my chest. My back burns where her hands are against my shirt. I pray she doesn't notice. We are just friends, that's all we'll ever be. That's all we can ever be. But her touching me doesn't help the images that were in my head earlier.

"Come on, you weirdo," she says after a second. "Don't leave me hanging, hug me back."

I force myself to move. I slip my arms around her and wish that the moment could last longer than a handful of seconds. That my hug could somehow take away all of her pain and make everything better. That it could mean something more than friends.

I swallow as I take a step back, knowing that I'm already falling for her, even if I shouldn't be. I can't seem to help it. Something about Annie just pulls me to her, and I don't want to make it stop.

☀

"Hey man, you think we could hang out after school, I don't have work today?" Noah asks as we walk down the hall to the lunchroom.

"Sure," I say, already scanning the hallway to see if Annie's heading toward the cafeteria or not.

"I've got to retake my math test now, but I'll see you later?" He turns before I can reply and heads toward the math wing.

Annie's bright orange-red hair snags my attention as soon as I walk into the cafeteria. She's at a table with Emily, a brown paper bag sits unopened in front of her and she's got her nose in a book. I can tell from here that it's a classic, I just can't tell which one. Emily doesn't seem to mind though, she's looking all gooey eyed at a guy who's wearing a football jersey. He's looking at her the same way and neither notice when I slide into the seat next to Annie.

"Hey," I say, and she looks up, her smile hits me straight in the heart. We haven't hung out a ton, since I spend more time with her brother than I do with her, but she's a familiar face—at school and lately in my dreams.

"Hey yourself," she says, and she reaches for her lunch bag and starts to open it. "No Noah today?"

I shake my head as I pull out my own sandwich. "He said something about having to retake a math test."

She smiles at me again and looks around the table then back at me. "Sorry about Emily and Landon, they just started dating."

I glance at the couple who are now so close to each other I half expect them to start making out right here. High school is weird, I can't wait to get out of here. I turn to Annie and as I move my hand across the table to grab a chip, my hand bumps into hers.

I notice, not for the first time, all of the freckles that cover her hand and move up her arm under her sleeve. I like her freckles; I like a lot of things about her.

"It's fine," I say, trying to shake my thoughts about how I like her freckles from my mind. This is Annie, my best friend's little sister. One of my friends. But no matter how many times I tell myself that, I can't shake the crush I have on her.

She laughs—a soft, sweet sound that makes my heart start beating faster in my chest. "It's not fine, it's awkward. I've told Emily this before, but she doesn't seem to care. All she seems to care about is if she can kiss whichever guy she likes this month and right now, that's Landon."

I glance at the two lovebirds who haven't started kissing—

thankfully—and look back at Annie. Her lips are a dark pink color and they look soft.

I cough and tear my eyes away. What is happening to me? Everyone has lips, why do hers make me feel something? Will they ever stop making me feel something? I have to get a grip.

I focus on eating my sandwich and she eats her food. The chatter in the cafeteria isn't overwhelmingly loud, but loud enough that it's fine we aren't talking.

"You two are so cute!" Emily's voice snaps me out of my own thoughts and I look up to see her beaming at us.

"What?" Annie asks, she sounds absolutely horrified. I don't dare look at her. "I don't date."

My stomach turns, I set down my sandwich, appetite gone. I know she said she didn't want us kissing, but I thought it was just because we barely knew each other, because we were brand new friends.

Emily laughs. "But you two would be so cute together. Sam is so tall and you're so short, it'd be so cute. Plus you both have gorgeous eyes. Your kids would be so pretty."

My mouth drops open but no words come out, I sneak a glance at Annie and she's refusing to look in my direction. Her entire face is red.

"Emily," she whines quietly and Emily just smiles.

"I promise I'm a good matchmaker, aren't I, Landon?"

"She is," he agrees, and I shift uncomfortably in my seat.

"We're just friends," I say, trying to make Annie feel less awkward. And we are just friends.

But friends don't think about how soft their friend's lips look and wonder what it would be like to kiss them, I tell myself but then shake away the thought. Annie and I are friends.

"Right," she says quietly, "we're friends."

Emily shrugs. "Okay, but I still think you'd be cute together."

"Can you please drop it?" Annie hisses at her best friend and I bite my lip. I like seeing her like this. She's normally so put together and nothing seems to phase her. But this, Emily's teasing, it's getting to her and I want to know why, even if I shouldn't.

Emily gives her a smile. "I'm making you uncomfortable, I'm sorry. I'll stop."

"Thank you," Annie says, and Emily goes back to flirting with Landon.

"I'm so sorry about that," she whispers to me a few minutes later. She's staring down at her sandwich and won't meet my eyes, her cheeks are still pink.

"It's fine," I tell her. "We are friends and she is obsessed with love, so she probably just wants you to date someone so that you two can double date or something."

"I don't date, and she knows that."

"Why not?" I ask.

She glances at me then looks away. "I just don't. I don't want a relationship."

"That's fine," I tell her as an ache I didn't realize was there starts to grow bigger inside my chest. "But I am glad we're friends."

"Me too."

I don't think about her reaction as I finish my lunch. I definitely don't think about how embarrassed she was from all of Emily's teasing, instead, I remind myself over and over that she doesn't want to date anyone, so all we can ever be is friends. Maybe someday I'll believe it.

5

———

ANNIE

June 2011 - Annie is 15, Sam is 16

I pick up and put down my phone three times before I type out a text to Sam. I set my phone down and hop off of my bed and pace my small bedroom. I don't know how much longer I can take sitting in my room. My mom just started dating a new guy who's at our house all the time. Which I guess would be fine if Mom was here too, but she's out with friends today so it's just me and the boyfriend who gives me creepy vibes.

It's not exactly an ideal afternoon. But Emily's out of town and Noah's at work. I think Sam is home, since his truck is in his driveway, but he and I haven't ever hung out alone before. We're always with Noah, Emily, or one of Sam's sisters.

I grab my phone and send the text before I can lose my nerve.

Me: Can I come over today? I need to get out of the house.

We're friends. Friends hang out. It shouldn't feel like a big thing, but I feel weird, texting only Sam and not having Noah around. That's the only reason.

He texts me back almost right away.

Sam: Sure! I'm not doing anything though.

Me: I'll be over in five. And that's fine.

I busy my mind by grabbing one of my canvas bags and look around the room to find something I can put in there. My gaze lands on the two cookbooks I just got from the library yesterday and *Little Women*, the book I've been reading again this week. I stuff them both in my bag, reassuring myself I'll feel more comfortable reading at Sam's house than staying here with Mom's creepy boyfriend.

I open my bedroom door slowly, because I don't want to talk to the boyfriend if I can help it. The TV is blasting at full volume and I breathe a sigh of relief. I quietly shut my bedroom door and tiptoe down the hallway and slip out the back door.

The summer air is hot and a little muggy, and just like usual, it smells like cows. It always smells like cows here on summer afternoons. I take in a big, stinky breath before walking across our weed-filled yard and into Sam's perfectly manicured yard. I've seen his mom and sisters working out in their garden in the mornings and wonder what it would be like to have a mom who cared about anything but herself.

I walk to the back of the house where Sam's room is and I tap on the window. He is lying on his bed with headphones in. He pulls them out and he hops up, looking at me in surprise. Because I probably should have gone to the front door like a normal person. He slides the window open and pops out the screen.

"Hey," I say normally, as if me crawling through his bedroom window is a normal occurrence. But this is so different from our normal.

"Noah working today?" he asks and I nod. When Noah has been at work this summer, I've spent my time hanging out with Sam—but always with one of his younger sisters. Amelia is twelve and Jodi is seven, so generally we play board games with them, but it's never been just the two of us.

"I was just watching some videos on YouTube about guys who travel and make videos about it," he says as he plops down on one side of the bed. I cautiously sit on the other, since his queen bed takes up most of the room and there is nowhere else to sit. But I've never been alone with him in his room before, let alone on his bed.

I glance at the closed door, "Will your parents care that I'm in here?"

He shakes his head, "Probably not. Plus, everyone's at the farm today. Amelia and Jodi wanted to go see what Dad does all day so Mom made a day trip out of it."

"And you didn't want to go?" I ask.

"Nah, farming is not really my thing. This though," he holds up his iPod. "This could be my thing."

"You're totally going to travel someday." I grin at him, relaxing a bit even though we're alone in the house. He feels like a giant teddy bear that would never hurt a fly, and I can already feel my heart rate slowing from being so nervous at home. I can't quite put a finger on why Mom's boyfriend gives me the creeps, but I know I need to trust my gut—and it is telling me not to spend another day alone in the house with him.

"I can see it now, Sam Holland, world traveler." I put out my hands as if there's a banner in front of me with the words.

"That would be cool," he laughs. "Though I might have to come up with a different Youtube channel name because World Traveler doesn't seem that exciting."

I shrug, "I didn't say I was any good at coming up with creative things."

"Unless it's food." His eyes seem to sparkle as they meet mine.

"Unless it's food," I say. "And speaking of food." I pull out the two cookbooks that I brought to flip through. "I've been learning about Italian food lately. I think I'm going to try and make my own pasta sometime soon."

"Very cool," he says, and then he puts one of his earbuds in and looks down at his iPod touch. We fall into a comfortable silence.

I read one of the cookbooks, studying the recipes that sound interesting and trying to soak in all the techniques I can without actually doing them. It's quiet and I feel content as I sit beside him on the bed. And it's better than wondering if Mom's boyfriend is going to try and talk to me or watch me like he always does which makes my skin crawl.

I head home about fifteen minutes before Noah gets home from work, and when he asks me about my day, I tell him I spent most of the afternoon reading, which isn't a lie. But it feels like I'm keeping a secret.

☼

Me: Mom's new boyfriend makes me uncomfortable

I slide my phone back into my pocket before Mom or her creepy boyfriend notices I had it out at the dinner table.

"You should get a job, Anne." The boyfriend grunts in my direction. I refuse to call him by his name, even in my head. He's been bugging me all summer to get a job and I don't know how many more times I can have this conversation.

"It's Annie," I say through clenched teeth as I take a bite of the pizza mom ordered for dinner. Noah is at work—he works as a clerk at the grocery store to help mom pay the rent because she never has money or a job. "I'm only fifteen, and school starts in two weeks."

I am counting down the days until school starts again. Mom and her boyfriend don't seem to do much except stay home and do who knows what all day long. Noah has been working more, which tells me he doesn't like this boyfriend either, and I've been hanging out with Sam.

Sam. My phone vibrates in my pocket but neither of the adults notices. Thankfully. If they did, it would probably be another thing to yell at me about. Instead, they are busy glaring at me about not wanting to get a job. I wish I'd had a part-time job over the summer, to at least get me out of the house. But I don't want all of my money to go to Mom and her boyfriend's drinking habits.

"You need to help your mom out with some of the things around the house now," Mom's boyfriend says and I suppress a shiver as his dark, dim eyes bore into mine. He's some sort of slimy salesman and while I don't like him, he must be a good sales-person, if Mom is dating him. He also must have some sort of money since that's the only type of man she seems to go for these days. Then she'll complain to them about how hard it is to work and how she wishes her teenage children would do more while she sits around and does nothing. Which makes me wonder why he wants Noah and I to take care of mom, if he's got money, why do they even hang out here? But for reasons I'll never understand, Mom always dates men like this, and they always seem to stick around.

Longer than I would if I was dating someone like my mom.

I barely hold in an eye roll as I look away. Minus tonight, I've made dinner for myself and the two of them every night this summer while Mom sits on the couch and does nothing. The only reason I do it is so I can learn how to be a better cook. I want to be a chef when I get out of here. I can't devour the cook-books they have at the library fast enough. I want to learn every-thing I can about food and cooking helps with that. Someday, I'll be a chef and I'll never have to come back to this house again.

"Just think about it, sweetie," Mom says in her soft, over-motherly voice she uses when she's got a newer boyfriend. This one has only been around for two months and is already acting like he runs the place.

He also tried to get into my room last night. I was up reading so I wasn't asleep yet and I heard him swear after he found my door locked. I have a feeling that he'll try again tonight, and he could easily get through my lock. But I'm not taking any chances. I'm not sleeping at home. Emily is out of town—again, her family has been traveling so much this summer—but I have another plan.

I ask to be excused and Mom says yes while her boyfriend tells her I have no manners. I put my dishes in the sink and head down the hall into my room. Locking the door behind me, I quietly shift my dresser to block the door. Now all I have to do is wait until Mom and the creepy idiot she picked go to bed or get drunk enough that they won't notice when I open my window to sneak out.

There's a reply from Sam when I pull out my phone.

Sam: Do you want me to come over?

Me: No. But I can't stay here tonight. It's a big ask, but could I stay with you?

Sam: My window will be open. Just tap once and I'll let you in.

He is risking a lot by doing this for me. I can't imagine his parents would react well to know he's inviting a girl into his bedroom while they're asleep. But it's my only option tonight.

Me: Thanks. I have to wait till Mom is asleep, my window creaks too much.

Sam: I'll be awake.

I pace my room, since reading a book will just be a distraction and I'll lose track of time. I don't want to keep Sam up too late if I can help it. But it's around ten when I finally hear Mom giggling as they walk past my room and into hers. The door shuts loudly and they turn on what I assume they think is romantic music. It just makes me want to barf.

I send a quick text to Noah so that he doesn't check in on me when he gets off work at eleven because I'm tired and going to sleep. Most nights I'm still awake and reading when his shift ends and we talk for a bit when he gets home. But I don't want him to freak out if he can't get in my room, that's the last thing I need.

Me: Going to sleep now, don't worry about checking in on me. I'll see you in the morning.

I slip my phone into the tiny pocket of my pajama bottoms and slide my window open as slowly as I can. It squeaks, just like I knew it would and I freeze, waiting for footsteps in the hall. But the house is full of Mom's terrible music. I could probably walk out the back door and she wouldn't notice, but I'm not going to risk it. I pop the screen out and climb out my window, grateful that we only have a one-story home. I close the window again, but not quite all the way so I'll be able to open it in the morning and slide the screen back on before walking across the yard and into Sam's yard.

His house is dark as I head to the back right window that's his. The rest of his family must all be asleep already.

I tap once on the window pane and it's as if he was waiting right there for me, the blinds slide up and I see him, backlit by the lamp that sits beside his bed. His window doesn't squeak as he slides it open and pops out the screen. I don't say a word until I'm safely in the room.

"Thank you," I whisper.

"Of course, Annie. Anytime," he says and I notice he looks completely exhausted. He goes to bed much earlier than I do and he probably stayed up for me. "I have a queen bed," he says awkwardly and I see his face turn pink in the dim light. "I mean.

I'm sorry. I don't want you to feel uncomfortable. There isn't room...for someone to sleep on the floor.

"The bed is fine for both of us," I hear myself say. I've suspected that Sam has some sort of feelings for me for a few weeks now, based on how he looks at me—like I'm the only person in the world he wants to look at—and I don't want to give him the wrong idea, but I can't be home tonight.

He nods, one time before crawling onto the left side of the bed. I climb onto the right, placing my phone on the nightstand. "Thanks, again, Sam."

"Anytime," he says before he turns off the light.

We lie together in the bed in silence. I wait for my heart to start racing—I'm sleeping in a bed next to a boy—but it doesn't. Sleep doesn't come either, so I try to focus on Sam's steady breathing, but instead, my mind wanders to last night, the twisting of my bedroom door—which I always keep locked—just after midnight.

"Annie?" Sam whispers, breaking up my memories.

"Yeah?" I breathe back.

"You're shaking."

I honestly hadn't even noticed. I'm not sure who moves first, me or him, but one second I'm on my side of the bed shaking, and the next Sam is pulling me against his chest. His arms go around me, pulling me into a tight hug. My back against his chest. I feel his steady breath against my back as my body starts to relax and the fear eases from me.

"Thank you," I whisper again as I snuggle closer to him. I know I shouldn't encourage his feelings, but to be held like this? It's the best I've felt in a long time. "You make me feel safe."

"I'm glad," he whispers against my hair. He's got an arm over my chest, his hand clutching my shoulder, keeping me against him. Our legs are close, but not touching. I close my eyes, feeling calm for the first time all day.

"Annie?" he asks a few minutes later.

"Yeah?"

"You're like sunshine, don't let anyone ever dim that light."

I blink my sleepy eyes, trying to not fall asleep. "Hmm?"

His voice is soft and low as he whispers in my ear, "You just keep showing up every day with a smile on your face, even when things are crappy. I really admire that. You inspire me. You're my sunshine."

I nod in response. Sleep is coming fast now and I don't really have time to process the words he just said. I have never felt so secure and safe as I've fallen asleep and I can't seem to fight it. When I'm on the edge of consciousness, I feel Sam shift, pulling me closer. And I know it's only my imagination when I feel his lips press against my hair.

6

———

SAM

July 2012 - Sam is 17, Annie is 16

"Shouldn't we go do something?" I ask. Noah is lying on his bed, flipping through a college brochure and wondering whether or not the college he picked is actually a good pick for him. "You already got in. You don't need to be doing this."

"But I just need..." Noah starts, but I can't sit still anymore.

I jump up. "Come on, man. Let's go see if Annie is doing anything with her friends today."

Noah gives me the look that I've been getting every time I suggest we hang out with Annie and her friends. I told him that I liked her friend Emily because I couldn't tell him the truth—I'm falling in love with and will probably always love his sister. I'm fairly certain that Annie knows exactly how I feel, but I haven't told her. I've never been exactly good at hiding my feelings, and the two of us have hung out a lot over the past year.

I know she's not interested in dating anyone, ever. I'm not dumb enough to believe that I could be an exception, but I can't seem to get my feelings to go away so I've stopped trying. I am in love with someone who will never love me back. Since I just graduated and I don't know where life will take me yet, I'm trying to spend as many days with Annie as I can this summer.

"I think Annie said she, Emily, and Lainy were going to the bowling alley in Greeley today," Noah says, still looking at the pamphlet on his bed.

Perfect. I snatch the paper away from him. "Okay, let's go see. I'm tired of sitting around. I'll even drive."

It's true, I don't like sitting around. That's the exact reason I'm putting off college for another year. I'm going to travel and start a vlogging YouTube channel before I decide what I want to do for school. See if traveling sparks any ideas. Wait and see where Annie ends up going to college, in a friend's kind of way.

"Fine." Noah sighs. "But you owe me."

I slap his neck as he stands up. "Owe you for what? Saving you from being glued to a college brochure all day?"

"Annie!" Noah yells as soon as we're out of his room, ignoring my comment. She appears in the hallway wearing a long, yellow sundress that's sleeveless. I wish I could count—or kiss— the freckles on her arms and shoulders, but if I told her or Noah that, they'd probably think I was a creep. Maybe I am a creep. Friends don't think those kinds of thoughts about their friends and I can be her friend.

She's also got her nose in a worn copy of *Emma*, her favorite classic. "Hmm?" she asks, not even looking up at us.

"When are you going bowling?" Noah asks her.

"At one," she answers, without taking her eyes off the page.

I glance at the clock on my phone. "It's twelve-thirty now"

"Okay," she says.

An awkward silence fills the hallway. Noah jumps in when I don't say a word. "Can we come?"

I give him a thankful smile and look back at her.

She eyes both of us, but her gaze settles on me, warming me from my head to my toes. "Are you bored?"

"Extremely bored, sunshine." I love how her cheeks flush slightly at my nickname for her. It's still new, but I like using it. The feeling I get knowing I flustered her slightly is a high I'll be riding for weeks.

"Sam wants to hang out with Emily," Noah says and I see her smile dim slightly for a second, but then she's back to her usual happy self.

I wonder if I should tell her the truth. I wonder if it would change anything.

I didn't say I wanted to hang out with Emily, but if I can keep Noah's suspicion off where my desires truly lie, all the better. At least until Annie graduates. Then it won't matter, because she'll be an adult and out of her mom's house. And I'll officially be an adult too. Being the youngest in my grade has always bothered me, but that's what happens when your birthday is at the end of July. But right now, I don't care as much, because I'm still only seventeen.

She rolls her eyes. "Of course he does. You guys can come, but Sam has to drive."

"Sure thing," I say.

Ten minutes later, we're all piled in my truck. It's days like this I'm grateful I can lift up the center console to create another seat. Annie is squished into that extra seat next to me with Emily in the passenger seat. Noah, Lainy, and Lainy's younger brother are in the back seat. Annie still has her book out.

"Will you please put that away?" Emily asks her. "I thought you said you wouldn't bring a book."

"I'll leave it in the truck," Annie says as she flips a page. I need to read *Emma* so I have some sort of idea about why she loves it so dang much. She reads it multiple times a year.

"I'm glad you guys came," Emily says, looking at me and then back at everyone in the back seat. "It'll give me someone to talk to when Annie brings her book inside the bowling alley."

"I'm going to leave it in the truck," she exclaims, but she isn't fooling anyone.

When we get to the bowling alley, I turn off the truck and grab the book from Annie's hand.

"Hey!" she says reaching for it. Her shoulder brushes mine and I get a whiff of her strawberry shampoo. It nearly undoes me, but I manage to keep my composure.

"You said you wouldn't bring it inside," I tease.

"Go, Sam!" Emily cheers as she gets out of the truck. Noah gives me a smirk over her shoulder as he watches from outside. He thinks I'm doing this for Emily.

"I'll put this in my pocket for you," I say, and Annie stills.

"Really?"

"Sure," I say. "If things get too boring, I'll give it back to you."

"Alright." Annie follows her friend and slides away from me and out of the truck.

I get out and slip the small novel into my back pocket. It's way bulkier than my phone, but it's fine. I feel like I've got a little piece of her with me, and I'm not sure I want to give it back.

Once we're settled in our lane, Noah says, "Annie, let's go order some food."

She scrunches up her face. "Didn't you just eat lunch?"

"Come on," Noah says and I give him a nod as if to say thanks, even if I don't mean it.

I watch as Annie grumbles but follows Noah to the small concession stand.

"I know you like her," Emily says.

My head whips around to face her. "Wh-what?" I stammer.

Emily smiles at me. "Noah told me that you have a crush on me. I just smiled and went along with it, because while I'm flattered by the rumor, it's obvious to anyone with eyeballs that you care about Annie." Then she frowns. "Except maybe the Jones siblings. Neither one of them seems to have caught on."

"Thankfully," I murmur.

"So I was right?" she asks.

I nod. "You gonna tell her?" I ask her, worried.

She shakes her head. "No, but you should."

I want to ask why, but Noah and Annie return with a tray full of nachos and pizza.

"We're going to eat nachos while we're bowling?" Emily asks with a raised eyebrow. "Like we're putting our fingers in those bowling balls that probably haven't been sanitized ever and then you're just going to eat?"

Annie groans. "This food is garbage anyway. I could have made us something if I'd known you'd wanted to eat."

I point to her. "We should have let her make us food."

Noah just laughs. "Come on, greasy pizza and gross nachos are fun sometimes."

"I cannot believe we're related," Annie says as she watches Noah dip a chip into the nacho cheese—or whatever it is. Annie has always been a bit of a food snob. She always wants to eat the best things. But after taking a cooking class her freshman year, she started cooking at home and making up her recipes and they taste pretty good. Which is nice, since my mom doesn't cook very well and Annie and Noah's mom works a lot so she's not usually home for dinner.

"Mmmmm," Noah says. Annie rolls her eyes.

"I'm gonna bowl." She stands and grabs the six-pound ball, the smallest one they have, and it still looks too big for her and her petite frame.

I try not to be obvious as I watch Annie bowl, but Noah is distracted by his nachos so I watch her as she bowls a seven and then doesn't hit any more pins.

When she returns, she sits in the empty chair next to me.

My heart flips like it always does when she's close to me. "Can I have my book now?"

Emily throws her hands up in the air. Lainy laughs—her and her brother are quiet additions to the group. Both of them seem to like observing more than talking.

"What" Annie asks her. "Everyone has to have a turn before it's my turn again, why can't I read?"

"Because we're hanging out," Emily says as she stands and grabs a bowling ball. "We should talk and have fun and live a little in the real world."

"Not giving you your book, not yet," I tell Annie, and she rolls her eyes like she's mad at me, but I see her smirking.

"Yeah," Noah says. "You ladies should tell us which guys you want to date next year and we can tell you if they're any good or not."

My stomach sinks. Noah has always been a bit of a romantic, he loves the idea of love. He and Emily really should go out, because she seems to be the same as him.

"Yeah right," Annie says and I notice her whole face is pink. "Like I would tell you who I like."

Emily comes back from bowling a strike.

"So there is someone!" Noah says. "Do we know him?"

Annie brings her fingers to her lips and locks it like she has a key. "Nope. Not gonna happen."

Lainy looks between Annie and I before getting up to bowl. My stomach swirls. Does Annie like someone? Does she like *me*? Could it mean she's going to change her rules about dating and romance? These questions rattle my brain for the rest of our game.

After we finish bowling, we head over to the mini arcade and play a few games. Noah loses every single one that he plays and Annie only wins two tickets. I end up with a motherload.

"Come on," I say to Annie. Emily is on the phone with her mom. "Let's go pick out a prize."

She holds up her two tickets. "I'm pretty sure this won't get me anything."

I hold up my stack. "My treat then." She tucks a loose piece of hair behind her ear and I expect her to refuse because I know she knows thanks to Noah that 'I like Emily' but she follows me.

"Pick anything you want," I say as we look at the display case. I watch as her eye catches on a fake gold ring with a sun etched into it. She turns away from the case.

"Surprise me," she says before reaching her hand to my lower back pocket and swiping her book. "I'll be over there."

I watch, frozen, as Annie returns to our table and opens up her book.

"I'll take that ring, please," I say to the kid behind the counter. He doesn't even reply before handing it over.

I walk slowly over to Annie, playing with the ring in my fingers. I assume it's probably against some rule for a guy to give a girl who is supposed to only be a friend a ring, but I don't care.

I hold it up in front of her nose. "Here, sunshine."

She grins up at me as she takes the flimsy ring from my hand, our fingers brushing in the process. "Thanks, Sam," she says quietly, as she slips it onto her thumb, the only finger the ring fits.

I want to say something clever, but Emily comes over. "My mom is throwing a fit about how I need to come home and clean my room, so can we head back now?"

"Sure," Annie says. I'm sure she's not in the slightest disappointed that she gets to go home and get back to reading. "Noah, let's go."

We're all fairly quiet on the way back. I drop Emily off first, then Lainy and her brother, before pulling my truck into my driveway.

"See you later?" Noah asks as he hops out.

"Sure, man," I say.

"See you," Annie says quietly. "And thanks for the ring."

She slides out of the truck without another word.

I don't notice until she's already at her house that she left her book on the seat.

I stuff it back in my pocket, and promise myself I'll give it back to her before I take off on my first camping adventure and that I'll just read it to see why she loves it so much.

In the end, though, I don't ever give her the book back. I keep it, reading the parts she's got marked over and over and trying to understand her more.

I don't say anything about it and neither does she.

Just like neither of us talks about how she wears the ring for the rest of the summer. The fake gold glints on her thumb every time I see her.

I try to tell myself that it means nothing, but I think it means something. But we never get a chance to talk about it before I head out of the state and she starts her junior year.

7
______

ANNIE

July 2014 - Annie is 18, Sam is 20

I slip out of the house quietly. Noah has moved back home over the summer to save money. He's been living in an apartment in Greeley with Sam while he's been doing school online. Though Sam seems to be out of the state more than he's in it these days. But I saw Sam's truck at his parent's house last night. It's still there this morning and I can't wait to tell him the good news. I haven't told anyone yet, not even Emily. I want Sam to know first.

The morning sun is shining as I slip around to the back of his house. His dad left for work an hour ago and I know his mom is probably getting his sisters ready and out the door for whatever fun, summer activity she has planned—that woman knows how to stay busy. I quietly rap on the window of his room. A minute later, the blinds slide up, revealing Sam and his messy morning hair. He's groggy, but grins at the sight of me as he slides open the window.

"Hey, sunshine. A little early isn't it?" He yawns and I help him pop out the screen so I can climb inside.

"Yeah, I just couldn't sleep," I tell him as I enter his bedroom. Since he's been traveling a lot, I haven't been here in a while, but it feels like stepping back in time. His blue comforter that he's had for years is rumpled on the bed. The only thing that's changed is that there are more pictures of me, Sam, and Noah on the walls. None of us expected Sam's parents to stay in Kersey as long as they have, but apparently, they decided it was a good place to settle after years of moving from place to place. Sam might be Noah's friend, Noah's best friend, but we have had this almost secret friendship all the years he's been here. I spent many summer days and afternoons after school in this room.

The queen bed takes up most of the room and I crawl onto it as he shuts the window. He lays down beside me, but I'm sitting because I'm too wired to relax.

"What's up, sunshine?" he asks quietly. He doesn't reach for me, not that I expect him to, but there's a part of me that wishes he would. I know he had a girlfriend for most of this past year, a lady who traveled with him on some of his adventures for his vlog. I wasn't able to watch those videos because it's weird to see him with anyone else—it feels like he's mine, even if he isn't actually mine. Not like that. He's never told me his feelings, and when he started dating someone else, it hurt that he'd moved on, even though we're just friends. But we still text nearly every day and talk on the phone about once a week.

This news deserves to be told in person. "I got in!"

He sits up, grinning at me. "I knew you would! New York City here we come!" He holds out his hand to give me a high five which I gladly give him. His fingers wrap around mine though and I don't pull away. We're awkwardly holding hands, but I don't question it or let myself think about it.

"I wasn't sure I would. I also got accepted for a partial scholarship, so I'll still need to find a place to live and a job to help cover the rest of my expenses, but I'm going to culinary school." Saying the words out loud feels surreal. I got into my dream culinary school. I'm getting out of Colorado. I'm going to make the life I want for myself, whether my mom approves or not.

"You'll figure it out." He squeezes my hand. "And I could make my homebase New York City. We could get an apartment..." he trails off as his eyes meet mine. I feel like he's looking into my soul. He blinks and looks away. "As friends, I mean."

I nod. I knew what he meant. Sam knows I don't do relationships. I don't do one-night stands or dates. It's just easier to avoid it all rather than follow in the footsteps of my mother.

"You don't have to uproot your whole life for me." I give him a sad sort of smile. I've known Sam for four years now, but it feels as though I've known him my whole life. I've always known that at some point we'll have to say goodbye. At some point, I'll need to let him go so he can find someone who wants to settle down because I know that he wants the picket fence, to grow old with someone, and a life with lots of kids, and I can't give him that. I've been guarding my heart from completely falling for him because I can't give him what he wants. I also know it would be so easy to let myself love Sam, to let myself feel all the feelings I keep locked away. But, I can't. It wouldn't be fair to either of us.

He looks at me as if what I've just said was the stupidest thing in the world. "I travel over six months of the year, you'd have the apartment mostly to yourself unless Noah comes too."

"Which he would." I hold back the urge to roll my eyes. I love my brother, but his constant need to take care of me is getting old. I'm eighteen now, at some point he has to let me spread my wings and stop trying to be a father figure to me. He has to stop trying to protect me from Mom. I can leave now.

Sam laughs. "He probably would. I mean, I bet as soon as he finds out you got in he'll suggest that we move out there too, without it being 'because of you' so that he can keep an eye on you."

"I wish he didn't have to come," I say the words and immediately regret them as I watch Sam's eyes widen. It's not fair for me to do this, to keep him so close, close enough but never touching. Always just out of reach. But I can't let myself let him go. He's mine and that's selfish of me to keep him. But I promise myself that I'll let him go in a year, I'll have to. He's already twenty. He has his whole life ahead of him, and I shouldn't keep him so close to me when I know nothing will ever come out of it.

"Me too," he says softly. I wait for it to come, his confession of feelings, but like always, he is consistent and doesn't say anything. "Where is the school again?" he asks me as he grabs his laptop. "I can start looking at apartments."

"You'll do this with me?" I ask him and Sam looks at me as if to say, duh, I'd follow you anywhere. And my heart feels heavy because, of course, that's his reaction. "Okay," I say and then I squeal a little. "We're going to New York!"

Sam gives me that smile that's all mine. "We're going to New York, sunshine."

8

———

SAM

Two weeks later

Noah has called me three times in the past minute which lets me know that Annie told him the news. I also know that she's working today at the local diner so I'm going to have to deal with my best friend all on my own. He's been working a lot the past two weeks, which is why Annie hasn't told him yet.

Of course, this is probably better anyway. I already applied to a small two-bedroom apartment just a few blocks south of Annie's school. She assured me the size would be fine, as long as I didn't mind sharing a room with Noah.

I know it's probably the most idiotic thing I've ever done, offering to move to New York, finding an apartment for us to live in, all for a woman who won't ever let herself love me back the way I know she could. But I'm doing it anyway. Even if it means I end up with a shattered heart.

Now, I just hope that Noah suggests the move so he doesn't guess my true motives. He has never told me explicitly to not date his sister, but it seems to be an unspoken agreement—at least on his end—that Annie is his little sister and nothing more. I don't think he even knows how good of friends she and I are.

I call him back. He answers on the first ring. "Finally, man. I've been trying to get a hold of you."

"I can see that. What's up?"

"Can you come over? I need to talk to you about something important."

"Sure," I tell him. "I'll be over in a bit." Since I've been packing up my apartment already, I'm glad Noah asked me to come to him. It takes about twenty minutes to get to his house.

"Your mom home?" I ask as he opens the door. He shakes his head. "Out with a boyfriend or something." I know Annie hasn't told her mom yet about her news, she told me she was going to wait until right before she was leaving to do so because she knows her mom won't approve. And Annie will try to please her mom, even if it ends up wrecking her. So I fully support the choice to not tell anyone who isn't necessary until the cars are loaded up with stuff and we're about to leave.

"So, what's up?" I ask Noah.

"Annie's moving." He has no lead-up and he also shows no excitement over the fact that she got into culinary school.

I blink in surprise. "Oh?" I ask as if I haven't known this for weeks. Noah sits on the couch, running a hand through his hair.

He's stressed. "It's bad."

"Why?" I ask. I think everything about this move is a good thing for Annie. It will be a great way for her to start over and be away from her Mom who hasn't ever been able to say a positive thing about her daughter.

"She's going to culinary school," he says as if it's the worst thing in the world. "In New York."

"I mean, that's what she's been talking about for years." This shouldn't be that big of a surprise.

"But she's moving to New York. She'll be eaten alive there," Noah says, concern lacing his words.

"She can handle her own." It hits me at this moment that Noah doesn't know his sister that well. She's stronger than he thinks. She needs this more than he'll ever be able to guess.

"We'll have to move there," Noah suggests, just like we knew he would. I bite my cheek to hold back a grin. He won't ever have to know that I was planning to go to New York already. "But we can't make it seem like we're moving there just because she is. Could you make it your new homebase? Tell her you've always wanted to live in the city after living in upstate New York?"

"Yeah of course!" My reaction is a bit too enthusiastic.

Noah narrows his eyes at me, but says, "Thanks, man. Maybe you can move out there first and I can follow in a few months so it'll be less weird."

"Sure," I say. "I'll start looking into apartments." As if I didn't apply to one this morning.

"You're the best." He watches me carefully, as if wanting to see my reaction. "We've got to watch out for our sister."

Something swirls in my stomach and I feel sick. I should just tell him the truth. When I don't say anything, he pulls out his phone.

"Noah..." I start, then I take a deep breath because maybe it will be better if it's all just out in the open. I should have told her first, but I think she knows my feelings. Maybe if Noah knows, it'll make telling her easier. "I love her."

Noah doesn't react at first, he's looking down at his phone. "What was that?"

"I'm in love with her."

Noah blinks up at me. "In love with who?"

"Annie." I don't look away.

His face falls, morphing into confusion. "She'll never go for you, man. You're like an older brother to her," Noah says, trying to spare my feelings.

I don't tell him about the thousands of interactions Annie and I have had that tell me otherwise. I don't tell him about the lingering glances or extra touches that I know make us something more than friends. I don't say that she doesn't see me like a brother and never has, but that the real reason she'd never go for me has nothing to do with me, it's just how she is. But she's my best friend, and around her I can keep my feelings at bay, because when we're together we're just Annie and Sam, and nothing else matters.

"I just needed you to know," I say. "Before we do this, move to New York. I'm not doing it for you."

I wait for him to get mad, to tell me to leave Annie alone. Instead, he says something worse. "I don't want to see you get hurt."

I've already been hurt. Nothing hurts more than loving someone who won't fully love you back. But I can't kick these feelings—I haven't been able to for years. I don't reply.

"You should date other people in New York," he says. "Didn't you have a girlfriend for a while?"

I nod.

"Why did you break up?" He asks. "Was it because of Annie?"

"No," I tell him, and it's the truth. "Chelsea loved the traveling side of our relationship but hated it when we were home. She wanted to be traveling all the time, which is not something I can do. So she ended it."

Noah nods. "Find someone else."

It's not a threat because he doesn't want me ruining his sister or whatever, which would almost feel better than this. He's trying to spare my feelings. But I'm too far gone. My feelings have already been ripped to shreds and I'm still here, ready to bare my soul to Annie, even if I know she will never let herself want me like that.

"I'll try," I tell him.

Noah nods like this is the best thing I've said all day.

"Good."

"Good."

9

ANNIE

Mid August 2014 - Annie is 18, Sam is 20

"We made it!!" I can't help but jump up and down in my seat as the New York City skyline comes into view. This is really happening, I'm going to culinary school. I'm going to live in New York. I feel like Taylor Swift would be so proud. I pull out my phone to turn on "Shake it Off" which is her newest single. I have a feeling I'll love "Welcome To New York" in a couple of months once her new album drops. But for now, this feels like a good anthem. I'm leaving behind my past—shaking it off if you will—and starting fresh.

"We made it." Sam grins at me. We've spent the past several days in his truck driving across the country to get here. I've got one suitcase in the bed of his truck and Sam has even less. It seems weird, to leave everything behind and start a new life—together—but we're actually doing it. "And I know you're about to play Taylor Swift, I'll allow it. Just this once."

Sam has never been a huge Taylor Swift fan, which is fine as long as he doesn't actually care if I listen to her music or not. I laugh and click play and the already familiar beats fill the cab of the truck. "We're really here. I'm really doing this."

"You sure are, sunshine," he says from behind the wheel. Noah will be joining us in a couple of weeks, but Sam volunteered to drive with me out to New York so I'd be there in time for the semester to start.

Right before we left, I told my mom that I was leaving. She was mad, just like I knew she would be. For a second, my mind goes back to a few days ago.

"You can't leave now, what will I do without you?" Mom screams as I throw my backpack into the front seat of Sam's truck.

"I'm going, mom," I tell her. There isn't anything in the world she could possibly say that would make me change my mind. I've been counting down the days for this moment since I was fourteen.

"But, Noah's moving to New York too. I thought that if he ever left, at least I'd still have you." Mom gives me an angry glare, and my insides twists. I have to say no to her. I am not going to stay for her. I hate that despite everything, all of her harsh words and insults, there is a part of me that wants to stay and take care of her—like she's asking for.

"I got into the culinary school of my dreams, Mom, I'm going. And we're leaving now." I take a step back and run into Sam's chest. His hands move to my shoulders as if to say he's ready to back me up if he needs to.

Mom rolls her eyes. "If you would stop being so obsessed with food and getting a career, you could find a nice husband and settle down here to help me out."

My heart tightens in anger, all of the parts of me that wanted to say leave my body in one breath. Help her out as in pay all of her bills and wake her up when she's drunk and passed out so she can get to work on time so she won't get fired. Again. I'm tired of being my mother's keeper.

"Mom, I'm eighteen. I'm not ready to settle down and have a family." I ignore Sam's warm grip that's still on my shoulders. I don't think about how good it feels to have his hands on me. I still don't want to settle down and have a family, not with the role model I've had, I'd probably just screw it up. But there's no telling that to Mom.

"So?" She asks as if what I've just said is completely absurd. "I married your father when I was nineteen, but I'd known him all through high school. You need to get married. You need to stay here."

"No." I stare her down. I think this is the first time in my life that I've used the word no as a complete sentence and it feels good. I am not backing down.

Mom simply stares at me with the look that has made me crumble at times, but today I won't. Today I'm leaving for New York City.

"We need to get on the road if we want to make it to Kansas City today," Sam says from behind me. "I'm sure we'll call some-time, Ms. Jones."

Mom simply huffs at Sam. If she had it her way, I'd marry him and stay here and make a dozen adorable babies. But Mom isn't going to get what she wants from me, not ever again. She's taken too much.

I lift my chin with my new found confidence. I'm starting over, I'm finally leaving this life behind. "Bye." I don't give mom a second glance as I climb into the passenger seat of the truck.

Sam walks around and climbs into the driver's seat. He turns the key in the ignition. "Ready, sunshine?"

"I'm ready," I tell him. And I don't look back.

"We can get the keys to the apartment in two hours, so where should we go first?" Sam asks me, bringing my mind back

to the present. I'm here. I'm in New York. I actually left. I wait for the ache to come—homesickness, missing the only home I've ever known—it doesn't come.

"Let's find some food," I tell him, as I glance out the window. We're stuck in New York traffic and all of the skyscrapers are taller than I expected. But I'm here, I'm actually here. I grin as I pull out my phone. "I've got a list of places I want to try."

"Perfect." Sam glances over at me and I meet his eyes. They are the perfect shade of blue. Like the sky in the summer on a clear day. Or what I imagine the ocean looks like. His gaze softens when I don't look away. When I'm with Sam, it's like we're in our own little bubble. I want to stay here forever, with him looking at me like maybe I wouldn't screw up a relationship like my mom always does. Like maybe his love would be enough to fix all of my broken thoughts. A loud honk from behind us makes me jump, and I look away.

Sam starts to drive again and I pull up my list on my phone. What just happened? We are friends, and he moved here so I didn't have to be alone *as my friend*. We can't be more than that. I try not to think about what it means, him moving across the country with me. I don't want to give him the wrong idea, but I also don't know how to live my life without him. I know it's not fair of me to feel that way, but I can't let him go. I don't want to let him go. So at least for today, I'll be selfish a little longer.

We end up at a fancy new restaurant—not far from where our apartment will be—called Austen's. The hostess leads us to a candlelit table for two. Glancing around I notice how out of place our shorts and T-shirts look. I drape the cloth napkin across my lap. "This place seems way too fancy, are you sure we can afford it?" I whisper across the table. "Even the napkin feels fancy."

"I just got my first five-figure sponsorship," Sam tells me. "We can afford it, at least we can today."

I can barely contain my excitement, but I do catch him watching me.

"What are you going to order?" he asks as we look over the menu. "I don't even know what half of this stuff is."

I laugh. I've been reading cookbooks since I fell in love with food when I was fourteen, but Sam doesn't know as much about food as I do. "The steak looks good, or the prime rib. Oh, I might get the duck." I've never tried duck. I have always wanted to, but Mom thought it was too much of a luxury and would have lost it if I'd ever come home with a duck to cook. "Yeah, I think I'll get the duck."

"I'll get the prime rib, then," he says and sets his menu down, grinning at me. "Just think, someday, you can be the head chef of a place like this."

I flush, because that's my dream. To be a head chef in a fancy place making delicious food for people. Food that people will remember for years after they eat it. "I'd love that."

"You'll do it," he tells me. "You're Annie freaking Jones. The best chef there is."

We order our food and the exhaustion from all our traveling starts to hit me. "What should we do after this? You're going to have to keep me awake because I'm going to pass out while walking."

"You should have slept in the car today," he scolds. "I knew you were tired."

"I didn't want to miss getting to the city."

"I would have woken you up," he says. "I know how much this means to you. I wouldn't have let you miss it."

"Thanks, Sam." I run my hands over the soft napkin in my

lap. "Where are you going on your next trip?" With a new sponsorship, that must mean he'll be leaving again soon.

"I'm going to Japan," he says. "I haven't been there yet, so I'm really looking forward to it. My sponsorship is for a new Airbnb type thing that is opening over there, so no camping for me."

A lot of the trips Sam goes on are hiking and camping trips. He loves backpacking and hopes to backpack through Europe someday.

"Sleeping in a bed will be nice, right?" This past week was the first time I ever left Colorado. We hit a few famous stops on the way from Colorado to New York, including some food pit stops that were on *Diners, Drive-Ins, and Dives* just so I could say that I finally tried it. But I can't imagine what it would be like to go to Japan. I've never even been on an airplane.

"Right." He smiles. "I'll be there for two weeks, then I've got a few trips on the East Coast planned for this fall. I've heard it's beautiful here."

"Cool," I say. I'll mostly be busy with school and work—once I get a job—that I probably won't see him all that much, even though we'll be living together.

I lean back in my chair, the exhaustion of all the travel hitting me and we fall into a comfortable silence until our food arrives and it looks even more amazing than I could have ever imagined. The duck melts in my mouth at the first bite. And Sam moans in pleasure as he eats his prime rib. "I think you have to work here someday, just so I can come and eat this good food that was made by you."

"I could just learn how to make this food," I tell him.

"If you do, I'll think I died and went to heaven. This is freaking amazing."

I smile, happy to have converted him into a food lover.

There's just something incredible about food that is made with love and that is delicious.

"I don't think I need to eat for a week," I say as we step out into the New York summer heat. "That was so amazing."

"Agreed," Sam murmurs. "I'm so full but I could not stop eating. Where to next?"

We end up back in the truck, since there's only two hour parking at the restaurant and drive slowly through the city toward Central Park. A New York staple.

"This is incredible! I can't believe we're actually here," I say for the millionth time as we take a walk around the park. We walk near the carousel and I take in all of it. It's amazing out in the middle of a city there's a park so big that it doesn't even feel like I'm in the city now. I'll have to come back for sure whenever I'm missing nature.

"I love how happy this makes you." I turn to look at him, pausing in the middle of the path. Sam smiles. "Seeing you like this, you seem so alive, I love it."

"I love it too," I tell him. "But it's not just the city. I'd be lying if I said the company didn't have something to do with it." I blurt out this last part and as Sam's eyes turn soft and tender as he looks at me, I wish I could take back my words. They might be the truth, but there's no future for us. I might feel something more than friendship for Sam, but I don't date. And yet, I can't seem to push him away either. I don't want to push him away, I don't want to keep him in the friend zone.

He takes a step closer to me. "Oh yeah?"

"Yeah." My breath hitches as Sam puts a hand on my waist and I watch as his eyes move to my lips.

"This okay?"

"Mhm." My mind is screaming at me but I ignore it. I know I should put a stop to this, but what if this is my only chance to be kissed by Sam?

He leans in closer. "Still okay?" he asks and I can feel his breath on my face. He smells like cinnamon gum.

"Yes," I breathe.

"Annie?" he asks and I'm slightly thrown by the use of my name and not him calling me sunshine, but I recover just in time for him to say, "I'm going to kiss you now."

I nod and he closes the distance between us. I never let myself daydream of this because I knew nothing but a broken heart would come from daydreams, but now I wish I had spent some time thinking about what kissing Sam—or anyone for that matter—would be like. I just ate the best duck in my entire life and didn't think life could get any better.

But I was wrong.

His lips are soft and warm and he wraps his arms around me as I kiss him back. The kiss is all him, soft and gentle. Tenderness in every touch. Full of hope and warmth and I want to melt into his lips. I pull back. We both blink in shock.

"I can't," I say suddenly. This was a bad idea. I shouldn't have let him kiss me, his lips are going to haunt me for the rest of my life because I'm not the kind of girl that he wants to marry. I'm not the kind of person who gets married and with Sam, well, that's where kissing will lead. "I can't."

"Come on, Annie," he whispers, a fierce look in his eyes. "I know you feel something between us too."

"We can't," I say again. "We're going to be living together. I'm going to school. I don't date."

"We could be friends with benefits," Sam says, but I can't do that. He wants more, he wants everything. I can't give that to him. I can't give it to anyone. I won't give it to anyone.

"I can't," I say as tears bubble up in my eyes. "I need you to date, to move on."

"Annie..." His voice cracks.

"No," I tell him, breaking eye contact before this completely rips me apart. I can't see him look at me as I break his heart. As I break my own. "We won't ever be more than friends."

10

ANNIE

August 2019 - Annie is 23, Sam is 25

There's a spring in my step as I make my way to my new studio apartment. I pull out my phone to call Chiara, my closest friend from culinary school. She's here in New York at culinary school from Italy. I hit call and walk up the first flight of stairs to my apartment.

She answers on the first ring. "Tell me you got the job!"

"I got the job," I laugh into the phone. It doesn't feel real that I just got hired to train to be the head chef at Austen's. It's where I've dreamed of working for years since I first got to New York and now it's happening.

"We have to go out to celebrate tonight. Wait, this weekend. I have my last test tomorrow and shouldn't stay up late," Chiara says.

"This weekend, for sure," I tell her, excitement bubbling up inside of me. "Mitch Austen is just like everyone says."

Chiara squeals. Mitch Austen is renowned in the culinary world of New York. He's the current head chef but just chose me to be his replacement because he's going to be opening new restaurants all over the city.

"Is he as beautiful as all the pictures?" Chiara sighs.

"Somehow, I think he's even more beautiful in person." My heart flutters in a way that hasn't happened in far too long. Yeah, my new boss is hot—or maybe I just think he's attractive because he's so talented. Either way, I'm lucky. "I'll have to introduce the two of you once I've been working there longer." He's a few years older than us, and totally Chiara's type.

"Oh, I love you! You are the best friend a girl could ask for. But I've got to run. Congrats though," she yells the congratulations part. "I'll text you so we can figure out plans to celebrate."

"Alright. Love you too," I tell her and then we both hang up the phone. I've got a stupid grin on my face as I head up the three flights of stairs to my apartment and unlock the door.

I pull out my phone and text Emily, because she needs to know the news, and I need to tell her all about my hot new boss. She and I aren't as close as we were in high school, but we still keep in touch.

Me: I GOT THE JOB!! And Mitch Austen is even more attractive in person than he is in any online photos.

I set my phone on the counter and pull out the pasta I made yesterday to reheat for my lunch. I'm buzzing with excited energy.

My phone vibrates, and I lunge for it, but it's a text from Sam, not from Emily. He knew I had my final interview today.

Sam: Any news yet?

He is somewhere out of the country, but I call him anyway.

"Hey, sunshine," he answers, and his voice is low and quiet like I just woke him up.

"Hey, I got the job!"

"Yes!" Sam shouts and I can hear him moving around. "I

knew you would. I can't wait to come eat at the famous Austen's and have my food cooked by the amazing chef Annie Jones."

I snort. "You can eat my food any time, you know that."

"I know. But going to the restaurant where you will be the head chef, that's incredible."

The awe in his voice makes me weak at the knees. I sit on my bed which takes up most of the space in my tiny studio. "I mean, technically it'll be another year or so until I'm officially the head chef, I'll be under the current chef's wing while he trains me. But that's why I got the job since I'm fresh out of culinary school and haven't worked anywhere yet. He said it'll be perfect so I can find my style."

"That's amazing, Annie." Sam says my name with such reverence.

"Celebrate with me when you get back?" I ask him. Before he answers, I hear muffled conversations from his side of the phone. "Who's with you?"

"Hm?" Sam asks, distracted. "Oh, that's Christina. She was just wondering who I was talking to. But yes, when I get back, I'll take you out to celebrate. Wherever you want."

"Okay," I tell him, ignoring the disappointment that crashes through me. Sam's got another new girl. I shouldn't be surprised. Ever since we moved to New York and I told him to date other people, he has been. It's been almost four years since I shut things down between him and I still struggle with it. But, I can't exactly be mad, he did exactly what I told him to do.

"Has Noah shut up about Tally yet?" Sam asks, changing the subject.

"Nope," I tell him. Every spring, Noah mourns the loss of this girl he met years ago. Saying his only regret was how idiotic he was in not giving her his number. "But it's almost summer, so maybe he'll come around and be fine again soon. I'm taking him to a Broadway show tomorrow to get his mind off of it."

"Good, good," Sam says, but I can tell he's distracted. "I've got to go. I'll call when I'm back in the States."

"See you."

"See you, sunshine."

My elation seems to deflate a little after I hang up the phone. Sam is still mine in the way he's always been, but it's different now. He's dating Christina, and she's there with him and it's morning. That has to mean something.

My phone vibrates again, this time it is Emily.

Emily: Girl, I knew you'd get the job. I also just googled your new boss *HEART EYES* I hope you become best friends with him.

I swallow thickly as I type out my response.

Me: I honestly can't believe that I got the job. And he is very, very attractive. All sharp lines and soft eyes. Gah. I'm pretty sure all of my co-workers are already in love with him. And I think I need a new guy best friend, just talked to Sam. He's got a new girl. I just called him and it sounded like he was just waking up and he was with her.

My phone rings a minute after I hit send.

"I'm sorry, honey," Emily says immediately.

I slump on my couch, appetite gone. "I don't know why I feel so weird about it. He's dated other women before. I'm the one who told him to date other women. I shouldn't feel this way."

"I know, but it's always going to be weird when he's with someone else. Everyone back in Kersey always thought it was going to be you and Sam who ended up together."

I let out a laugh but it sounds more like a gulp. "Whatever."

"It's true. I've seen the way he looked at you. That man has loved you for a long time." Emily tells me and my heart pinches.

"I think he finally took my advice to heart, he finally moved on." My voice sounds small, even to me. I shouldn't care so much. I can't give Sam the life he wants, and he should be able to be with someone who can give him that. "Maybe it's time I moved on too. Find a new crush."

Emily sighs, "Only if you're ready."

"I think I need to, so I don't break my own heart any more than I already have. Sam deserves to be happy."

"So do you," she tells me. I know she's right, I know that I really don't need a man to make me happy. But having a new crush would be good for me, healthy. A slow grin spreads across my face.

"I know the perfect new crush."

"Mitch?" Emily asks me as if she can read my mind. "Isn't he like a decade older than us?"

"So?" I ask. "It would just be a crush, someone I can dream about instead of Sam. It's perfect. Plus, he's only like seven years older than us."

I remember the stern smile that Mitch gave me after offering me the job, and how warm his hand felt when we shook hands before I signed the contract. I know better than to date my boss, but...at some point, he won't be my boss. Plus, it's just a crush.

"It's perfect," I repeat.

"If you're sure," Emily says, but I can hear the wariness in her voice. She doesn't think this is a good idea. I just have to convince her it will be.

"Trust me, I want to stay friends with Sam, like we've always been. I can't ruin that by letting any sort of feelings get involved. So this is perfect. I've got a new crush."

"I don't think it works that way." Emily sounds skeptical. Which makes me laugh, because growing up, she had a new crush every single week.

"It's the perfect plan."

I hear screaming in the background—she's got a two year old and a husband. She's got a life I've never even let myself want.

"I've got to go, you'll keep me posted about how the job goes though?"

"Yup, talk to you later." I hang up the phone and stare at the screen. "Perfect," I tell myself. A new crush. Someone to focus on so I can just be friends with Sam like we've always been.

11

SAM

November 2019 - Sam is 25, Annie is 23

"It's either her or me!" Christina yells. We've been arguing about this for weeks. I've been back in New York for three months—with Christina—and I haven't seen Annie at all. She doesn't even know I'm back in the States. We haven't celebrated her new job, and I hate that. But Christina thinks it's weird that I want to take Annie out to celebrate. I invited her to come with us, but she just said I was choosing Annie over her.

But Annie is my best friend.

My girlfriend doesn't like that.

"I'm so sorry," I say and she glares at me, this isn't how I wanted things to end, but once again, my relationship is coming to an end. I can't get any relationship to stick, no matter how hard I try. There's only one Annie. Maybe it's time to finally admit that, and be okay with whatever it is Annie will give me. Even if all I get is to be her friend, I'd still choose that over any relationship.

She throws a flip flop in my direction and misses by a few inches. "Do you love her?"

"In some way, yeah," I say because it's the truth. I do love Annie, she means the world to me. We may only be friends, but I'll always love her.

She throws her hands up in the air. "I can't believe I uprooted my life for you."

"Technically, I did tell you that you probably wouldn't like my lifestyle." A flip flop hits me square in the chest. "I deserve that."

"You do." Christina isn't a weepy person, she's all fire and rough edges. But I haven't seen this side of her. She's angry and about to throw a fit. She's like other women I've met and dated while traveling—she wants to be on the move. I warned her we'd be in New York for a few months, at least, and she assured me it would be fine. I even told her about Noah and Annie, but she can't seem to see that I'm friends with Annie and could still be with her.

I stand in silence as I watch Christina pack up the rest of her things. She gives me one last glance before leaving the room.

"I hope she's worth it," she yells over her shoulder, and then I'm alone.

I pull out my phone to text Annie, asking if she has time to come over later. Maybe we can finally celebrate and I'll tell her the truth, that my feelings aren't ever going away.

Annie: What! You're back in the city and you didn't tell me?!

Annie: I can come over around seven.

Sam: I'll explain everything later. See you then.

Part of me hates that we no longer share an apartment, but I'm so proud of Annie for making her own way and living on her own. Plus, it gives me two hours to get her flowers and shower before she comes over. I can't wait to hear more about what it's been like to work in the restaurant. She's texted a little about it but we haven't talked on the phone as much or in person, and I know it's my fault.

Maybe it's time to tell her how I really feel. I pick up a bouquet of peonies from a little shop around the corner, and put them in a fresh vase on the counter before I shower.

The hot water hits my shoulders and I start to relax. Before, when I told a woman that I was interested in her, I felt nervous. But telling Annie that I love her? That feels as natural as breathing.

I pull my still damp hair into a short man bun as I hear a soft knock on the door just before a key slides into the lock and unlocks the door. Annie runs straight to me and I pick her up and spin us around as we hug.

"You're back!" Annie grins up at me as I set her down and release her. "It feels like it's been so long."

I've been back for three months, but I didn't tell Annie I was back in the city. I know part of it is because of Christina, but if I'm being honest with myself I knew that if I saw Annie again I'd fall even more in love with her, and that wouldn't have been fair to Christina.

"It was my longest trip. Six months," I tell her. This part is true, but all of my timing is messed up. I often travel and then while I'm back home, my videos are going up on YouTube for weeks after I've been back so my followers don't actually know where I am. There are too many weird people, this is a way that keeps me and my team safe.

Annie nods. "I know, I've been watching all of your vlogs. What have you been up to? I know you've been doing shorter trips and things, but didn't you finished your backpacking trip ages ago?"

I shift on my feet. "Thanks for watching. Just relaxing and doing smaller trips."

Annie sits on the couch and tucks her legs under her. "Tell me all about them."

I sit next to her, and our knees brush. Annie is absolutely glowing. I've never seen her like this. Her smile is making me dizzy. "No, no. If you've watched all my vlogs, you know all the things already. I need you to tell me about what it's like being a real chef."

Annie's grin only widens. "It's everything I ever dreamed of. I can't wait to have my own place someday. To be the one making all the choices about the food and the dishes. But I love it. Every day I get to cook food for people who truly love eating food. It's the best feeling in the world."

Her happiness is contagious. "That's so incredible, sunshine."

Annie looks away at her usual nickname.

Alarm bells go off in my head. "What is it?"

Annie shifts and after far too long, she looks me in the eyes. "I met someone."

All of the air seems to rush out of the room. This is Annie, the love of my life, the woman who is meant to be all mine and she's met someone?

"Sam?" Annie asks when I take too long to respond.

"Wow." I force myself to smile. "That's great Annie, tell me about him."

Annie starts to talk and I hear her at first. "He's a really incredible chef. I'd seen photos of him before, so I knew that he was handsome, but I never expected him to like me as much as he did. I'm one of the youngest chefs in the past decade to be brought on to train to be a head chef in the next couple of years. All because Mitch saw so much promise in me. And he truly has been so professional, but then he started asking me if

I'd come do private lessons with him at his house, which I couldn't say no to. He's Mitch Austen and he wanted to teach me."

I give Annie a small smile, but my stomach churns as she continues. "Then, a couple of weeks ago, he asked me out. I told him that I don't date, but that I'm happy to hang out and be friends. He asked me out a couple more times, and I kept telling him that I don't date anyone and why, but then last week he kissed me..."

My ears start to buzz as she starts to tell me about their kiss, lighting up all over again and I realize that it's not just the work as a chef that's making her glow. It's this. *It's him.* There is a man out there that isn't me who is making her so extremely happy. I smile and nod but I don't take anything in. I feel like I'm going to pass out.

"We should go on a double date sometime, with you and Christina."

"Yeah," I manage to get out. I don't have the heart to tell her that Christina and I broke up. I can't tell her how I feel now. Not when she's just told me that she's dating someone.

Jealousy burns deep within me, but I push it down. I never expected Annie to date anyone, and I hate that it isn't me. But she's my best friend. I can be happy for her.

"Will you be in New York for a while?" she asks me and the roaring in my ears starts to die down now that she's not talking about *him* anymore.

"Not sure," I tell her the truth. Well, part of the truth. The full truth is that I've got an inbox full of requests from brands and companies begging me to start right away, but I haven't answered any of them because I wanted to see how tonight would go. But I guess I've got my answer, it's time to travel more. I can't be here and watch Annie fall in love. That will kill me.

I can be happy for her but from a distance. I'll travel the

world. I'll find someone new. It'll be fine. At least, I hope it will be fine.

"Are you okay, Sam?" Annie asks me quietly.

"Just tired from my flight," I say, which isn't true at all since I flew back to the city months ago. But a different kind of weariness is creeping over me.

"You sure?" She asks.

I shake my head a little. I can't lie to her. "No. I'm not. But I'll be okay." I hope.

"I didn't mean..." She starts to say but I hold up a hand to stop her.

"We don't have to do this Annie. I never actually told you how I felt. You never asked me to wait for you. I'll be okay."

Someday. When I'm eighty. Or dead.

Annie doesn't look convinced. "Come here," I say, holding out my arms and she falls into them. My heart might break into a million pieces. This is where we should be, her and I. But it's time to move on, something I should have tried harder to do in the past. Sure, I've had plenty of girlfriends, but they've never been something I thought would last. Annie hasn't ever been mine, not in the way that I want. It's time to let go of the dream.

"I didn't mean for it to happen...he's just so..." Her words trail off as she buries her head against my chest.

"Please, for the love of all that is good and holy, don't tell me how great he is. I can handle you being happy, but I can't hear about him," I whisper

Annie nods against me because in some sort of way she understands, and I simply hold her while my heart falls apart.

12

ANNIE

June 2021 - Sam is 26, Annie is 25

The first time I leave Mitch, I nearly call my Mom, which is how I know it's bad. I want to call her and tell her that she was the perfect example all these years of exactly what not to do. And instead of listening to my gut, I fell for a man who I thought loved me.

Turns out, Mitch loves power more than anything else.

After I clock out of work, I sit in the small lunch room that's reserved for me and the other chefs. It's late, so nearly everyone has already cleared out. My gut clenches as I hear footsteps in the hall, my shoulders relax when I see that it's my friend Chiara.

"You okay?" she asks me, coming in and grabbing her food from the fridge. I got her a job here at Austen's shortly after I started working here. We've both been working here for two years.

"I broke up with Mitch." My shoulders slump as I say the words. This is why I don't date. Breaking up hurts, but not as much as being with Mitch does. I can't believe I was so dumb and didn't see him for what he was sooner.

Her eyes go wide. "What, no way? What happened?"

He hit me again and then destroyed me with his words as he blamed me. "I just don't think it's going to work anymore. You know I always said that I wasn't the dating type." I tell her, because how can I tell her that her idol is a raging narcissist who likes to hit his girlfriend? No one would believe me.

"That sucks," Chiara says as she sits at the table across from me. She eyes my phone. "You going to tell Sam?"

I was thinking about it. I even opened his text thread. We haven't talked much since I told him I'd met Mitch nearly two years ago. I think I've seen Sam once in all that time. I secretly watch his vlogs—because Mitch was furious the first time he saw me watching Sam on my laptop—and he's been traveling a lot. He seems tired, but his subscribers love his videos. He's started doing tricks on bikes and skydiving and doing all sorts of risky hikes that make me sick to my stomach to watch. I'm afraid he's going to get hurt every time, but I watch every single minute. I can't seem to look away.

"Probably," I tell her.

Chiara sighs.

"What?" I ask her.

"Did you break up with Mitch because you're secretly pining after Sam?"

"What? No way!" I say, surprised that anyone would even think that. "He's my best friend."

Chiara looks at me knowingly. "He was your best friend. The two of you have hardly spoken in the past eighteen months and I know how much it hurt when he stopped talking to you."

I shrug my shoulders. "I told him I met someone, it's not my fault he got all hurt and ignores me now."

"No, but it still hurts."

I bite my lip because this isn't how I pictured this conversation going. "I'm sorry if Mitch takes out his anger about the breakup on the staff."

"I doubt he will. He's a professional. And haven't the two of you fought before? I didn't even know until you told me."

It's just like Mitch to act like everything is fine in front of everyone else, but change when it's just the two of us. "He might be upset this time."

He was upset when I told him I thought we weren't working any more. I shift and the bruise on my ribs makes me want to scream, but I don't make a sound. I've gotten good at pretending I'm fine—so good that most of the time I believe it myself.

"Are you going to take some time off?" Chiara asks me.

I nod. "Yeah, I'm going to go visit my Grandma in Utah for a week then I'll be back. Maybe it'll give him at least a little time to cool off."

Chiara tilts her head at me like she wants to ask the questions I wish someone would ask, that she of all people would notice that something isn't right. But she doesn't. "Have a good trip."

I give her my practiced smile, the one that shows everyone that I'm absolutely fine, because I am absolutely fine.

☼

"It's so good to see you, darling." Grandma Marsha wraps her arms around me and I breathe in her familiar scent of hot chocolate and old books. Or maybe that's just The Book Shop, her book store that she's been running for years. Either way, being in her arms feels a little bit like coming home—a feeling that I'm not all that familiar with.

"It's good to see you too, Grandma." I smile at her. I can breathe easier here, away from New York City. But I ignore the thought because for the past ten years of my life, I've been dreaming about opening my own restaurant in New York City and I'm not going to let my terrible ex ruin that dream for me. I can't open my place yet, because I don't have any money saved. But someday, someday, I'll be free from Mitch and living my dream in the city that I love.

"I've missed you." Grandma Marsha says and I look away. Noah visits more than I do. I haven't made time for it in the past few years.

"I'm sorry it's been so long," I tell her truthfully. "Work has been keeping me busy."

"Tell me all about being head chef. Is it everything you hoped it would be?" Grandma smiles at me and I relax a little. She's missed me, but she's not mad that I haven't come to visit in so many years.

"It's the best," I say, and then, like usual, I get lost in telling her about the dishes we've been making and how I've been able to have more freedom and experiment with the menu a bit, which has been fun. I don't tell her about how Mitch still hangs around a lot, even though he told me in my interview that he'd give over the reigns to me by now. I try not to let it bother me, but it does. Instead, I tell her about my plans for opening my own restaurant, once I can save enough money, which isn't exactly easy to do in New York City. I make decent money, but most of it goes to rent and food. I put any extra penny I have into my savings, but it'll be a few more years before I'm able to do anything on my own.

"How's Sam?" Grandma Marsha asks after a beat too long.

"Fine," I say, which I assume is true. He seems fine from what I've seen on his channel. Plus, he and Noah are still doing their yearly trip together and that seems to be going well. At least Noah still has Sam.

"You don't see him?" Grandma asks as if she knows more than I'll ever tell her.

"Here and there." I keep my answer simple. Truthful, it's easier that way. "He's not in New York much these days. Busy traveling and all."

"Hmm."

"What?" I ask, shifting uncomfortably under her gaze.

"You love him." That is all Grandma says.

"What? No." I mean, yes I do *care* about Sam, but I could never be with him, we don't want the same things and that wouldn't be fair to him to make him a fling or something short. He's looking for a lifelong commitment and I'd rather not have him at all romantically if I can't give him all that he wants. Mitch was a reminder of why I don't date. And while Sam is nothing like him, I won't be dating anyone ever again.

Grandma Marsha smiles at me. "Just don't wait too long to tell him." My eyes bug out. Are we having the same conversation? Grandma waves her hand. "But enough about boys and cooking, did you see the new *Emma* movie?"

I'm grateful for the change in conversation, but my mind won't stop swirling about what Grandma said about Sam.

13

———

SAM

July 2021 - Sam is 26, Annie is 25

"You have a bruised rib." The nurse who's dabbing my bleeding chest with a rag tells me. "But the doctor will confirm that. He'll also give you something for the pain."

I grunt in response.

I'd rather feel this physical type of pain than the ache that I constantly feel in my heart. I grit my teeth and push away the heartache that comes along any time I'm reminded of Annie. Though, how a bruised rib did that, I don't have a clue.

"And my friend?" I ask, wondering how Noah is doing, and where he is. My heart is still pumping fast and I'm sure my ribs will hurt a lot more when the adrenaline wears off. But for now, I'm alive. Is it bad that I kind of hate that?

First, a bear came into our camp and was digging through the food that I forgot to tie up. Then we were in that dang tree for who knows how long before I woke up on the ground, my ribs hurting like crazy and a fire burning close. Noah said he remembers seeing the lightning, but I don't remember anything.

Thankfully, we're in Colorado—a place that I'm familiar

with—and I was able to drive us down the canyon and to an emergency room, despite the pain. A near-death experience will do that to you I guess.

"He'll be fine." The nurse tells me as she puts the cloth she was cleaning off my blood on the tray next to me. "I think he has a broken arm, it's a miracle that the two of you are even alive."

I give her a tight smile.

Alison, who's on my film crew, recently asked me if I had a death wish since some of the tricks I've been trying lately have been getting a little bit riskier. I laughed it off and was able to convince her I was fine. And I am fine, but the adrenaline I feel, the fear that comes from jumping off a cliff or out of a plane is much more manageable than the hole that I seem to have in my heart.

I never worried about Annie finding someone, because for so many years Annie told anyone and everyone who would listen that she was never going to date because she didn't want to end up like her mom. But then she did date. And she picked him. The guy who makes Noah mad when he comes up in conversation. I've never met him and I don't plan on it. If I did, I'd probably punch him right in the face and Annie would probably hate me forever.

So I keep my distance, which makes my heart ache. But it's better than the alternative.

Maybe. I'm alive, but the woman I love is in love with another man.

So I keep doing risky tricks.

I clench my jaw shut. I have to stop thinking about Annie, pining after her like this isn't helping me at all.

Camping with Noah wasn't supposed to be risky. It's my week off. It was supposed to be fun. Just two friends drinking a little bit too much and drowning our sorrows, while ignoring the sorrows that even exist. It wasn't supposed to end up with us in the hospital.

It takes a few minutes after I knock on the door of my parent's house for a light to turn on and the door to swing open. Which, I should have expected since it's the middle of the night.

"Sam!" My mom gives me a giant hug. "What a surprise. What brings you here?" she asks as welcomes me into the house that I can't believe my parents still live in. After moving around for so many years my parents finally settled in a small farming town. They still love it nearly twelve years later. "I thought you were camping."

I wince a little as she lets me go, my broken rib screaming in pain. "There was a fire," I tell her, which is the least bad thing of our night. "So we came home." It's easier to tell her that than to tell her the whole truth. I don't exactly need my Mom worrying about my hurting ribs.

"I'm sorry. I know you were looking forward to it," Mom says. I'm exhausted from not sleeping most of the night, but I still follow her into the kitchen and accept a cup of tea that she made.

"How are you?" Mom asks me and I give her my easygoing smile. At this point, I'm a pro at smiling at telling everyone that everything is good.

"Good, good. Things with the channel are great and in a couple of weeks I'll be heading to Europe again for the next year."

Mom frowns. "I wish you could do more of your backpacking trips here in America so we could at least see you once in a while."

I keep going to other countries because I can't risk running into Annie, and that will happen if I'm too close to New York. I'll go back. She's like a magnet, always pulling me to her.

"Maybe you and Dad could come out for Christmas. I'll pay for the trip." I rush to add before Mom complains about the expense of a trip to Europe.

"We'd like that," Mom tells me and she squeezes my hand. She then gets the look on her face and I know she's about to ask me about my love life and I'm not sure I can handle that right now.

"Well, I'm really tired, I think I'm going to get some sleep and we can talk more later."

"Alright." Mom gives me a sad smile like she knew that this was coming. I nod once and head down the hall to my room.

Opening the door and stepping inside feels a little bit like stepping back in time. The room is the same as it was when I was in high school. There's a picture of Annie and I on my nightstand which I move so it's facing down. Lying on the bed I stare up at the ceiling, memories flooding my mind of Annie sneaking into my room for the first time when her Mom's boyfriend was being a creep. That was the only time I slept with her in my arms.

I turn on my side, pushing the memories out of my mind. I've got to move on. I never did understand why Noah wallowed so much about the girl he met one time, but I guess I get it a little bit because I've spent the past few years of my life wallowing about Annie. It's time for me to grow up, to get serious. To find someone I can build a family with, make new memories with, someone who will actually love me back.

ANNIE

August 2022 - Annie is 26, Sam is 28

Work is good. Work is great. I'm the head chef of Austen's—finally—and I should feel amazing, but instead, I feel empty. I go through all of the motions tonight, waiting for the moment I can head home and watch reality cooking shows.

Cooking has always brought me so much joy, but tonight all I can think about is my relationship that is the exact opposite of a fairytale.

Mitch and I have been off and on again for the past year. He's like a drug I can't seem to quit. It doesn't matter what he does—the bad things—his stupid smile and charming, charismatic eyes always seem to bring me back. That and his subtle manipulation. I can see how he gets me everytime, but it's been almost a year since he last hit me, so things are going better. He really is changing. At least, that's what I tell myself even as I flinch every time I see his eyes get dark and angry. But the only thing he's hit me with within the past year has been his words. For now, I can live with that.

Plus, it helps that he's not at Austen's much these days. For the past two months, he's been working with contractors to get his next restaurant up and running. His days are full of paperwork and blueprints while mine are full of cooking the sauce the duck sits in and having customers tell me they'd like to bathe in it.

I should be on cloud nine, but I'm not.

Plus, my phone is burning a hole in my bag.

"What's with you today?" Chiara asks while we clean up the kitchen after closing.

"Nothing," I tell her. But the truth is, for the first time in over a year and a half, Sam texted me. I don't know what it said. I'd just clocked in and was putting my phone in my bag when I saw the notification so I've been wondering what he said for the past eight hours.

"Okay, weirdo."

I give her a nod, as I head out into the smoggy summer air. Instead of heading to Mitch's place where I've been living for the better part of two years I turn right and head to Noah and Sam's place. I know Sam is somewhere out of the country, at least I think he is, and Noah is visiting our Mom. I want to be alone though, when I read Sam's texts. It's been a long time since Mitch picked a fight about Sam, since Sam and I don't talk much these days.

But I'm not in the mood to argue with Mitch. I'll have to delete the texts later, but it'll be worth it. To get a night of relief. I need to end it, but I don't have the courage anymore. As I walk up the stairs to the third-floor apartment, the same one I lived in when I first moved to New York, I send a text to Mitch letting him know I won't be coming home.

Me: Hanging out with my brother tonight, see you tomorrow.

He doesn't know that Noah is out of town and he has no way to verify that what I'm saying is true. Mitch has never been to this apartment because he thinks the apartment building is too run down for him. When I told him I had lived in this building for years while going to culinary school, I'm pretty sure he about died. He's *established*—his word, not mine—and told me that someday we could buy our own penthouse together, instead of the one I've been staying at.

His reply comes in seconds later.

Mitch: working late anyway.

I sigh. If the roles were reversed, he'd be mad by that response, but I'm grateful. He's distracted and that's always a good thing. It's one in the morning and I'm ready to sink into the comfortable leather sofa in front of the TV before I fall asleep.

I slip the key into the keyhole and turn the lock, blinking in surprise at all the lights that are on.

"Noah?" I call out as I set my stuff out on the counter. Maybe I will actually hang out with him so my lie to Mitch won't be a lie. This makes me feel a little bit better.

I hear the shower running in the bathroom, so I make myself comfortable on the couch and pull out my phone. I let out a slow breath before going to my unread text from Sam.

Sam: Hi. Been thinking about you lately. That's never a good thing, but I was and wanted to tell you.

I stare at the text for a beat. After so much silence between, I'm not sure what to even say back.

Me: It's good to hear from you :) Sorry about the thinking thing though, that doesn't sound fun.

There. I can be fun and we can have a conversation. Maybe I shouldn't have sent the smiley face, but I can't edit the text, because it shows that Sam's read it.

Sam: What are you up to tonight?

I'm surprised that he replied so fast. I turn on a Gordon Ramsey cooking show before I reply.

Me: Currently sitting on your couch watching TV. Waiting for Noah to be done in the shower so we can hang out. You?

Sam: Just got up. Getting ready.

Me: Where are you right now?

The bathroom door swings open, and I'm about to call out to Noah so I don't freak him out when Sam appears in the hallway in nothing but a towel. I stare at him openly—I'm completely gawking, but I can't seem to look away—blinking twice and opening my mouth to talk and then closing it again. He's here? His hair is pulled up in a bun, but it's still wet. His beard has water droplets on it. I lick my lips and look away, feeling guilty. I've got a boyfriend. I can't feel *any* sort of attraction toward Sam. I swallow thickly.

"I'm here," Sam says softly and my eyes snap to his. "Noah isn't here. He's in Colorado for the week."

My eyes leave his—my first mistake—and I take in his chiseled chest. I wonder what it would feel like beneath my fingers. I close my eyes to shut out the image of his perfect body. "Can you put some clothes on, please?"

"You like what you see?" Sam asks in a teasing voice. Well, I think he's teasing because of the lilt at the end, but it also sounds flirty. That can't be right, not if it's directed at me. He's talked like that, low and husky, to other women. I've heard it on his channel. I heard it in this apartment when I was hiding away in my room. But never, never has he spoken to me like that.

"Just put some clothes on, Sam," I yell, my eyes still closed.

I swear I can hear him smirk as he turns and a few seconds later the door to his bedroom clicks shut. I open my eyes and wipe my sweaty palms against my jeans. What exactly is Sam doing here? How come he didn't tell me he was back? I glance at my phone, willing Mitch to text or call—to see through my lie—but my phone stays black.

When Sam returns to the living room, he's fully clothed but his hair is still damp and now that I know exactly what he's got hiding under all of those clothes, I'm not sure I can handle looking at him. So I close my eyes and go through my new alfredo recipe in my mind. Extra parmesan. Cream. Butter. Loads of garlic. Fresh parsley. It's nothing special, but it's delicious. I think I've finally perfected the combo of ingredients.

Sam snaps his fingers in front of me.

"What?" I look up at him. I zoned out enough that I didn't even hear what he said.

"I asked what you were doing here. In my apartment," Sam says as he falls next to me on the couch. There's about six inches between us, but that distance is lined with gasoline and I'm a match ready to catch fire and burn us both.

My cheeks burn. "I just wanted to be alone."

Sam tilts his head to one side. "Trouble in paradise?"

"You could say that," I say with a forced laugh. Sam's eyes turn serious and my stomach flips. "I just wanted to be alone," I repeat. "Why are you back?"

"Trip was over." He closes his eyes. "I'm only here for a few days."

"Great."

He is so close that I could reach out and touch him if I wanted to. I curl my hands into fists so hard that I know my nails will leave marks in my palms.

He settles into the couch and without opening his eyes, he says, "We should go out, catch up."

I swallow the bile that rises in my throat. If Mitch ever found out that Sam even suggested that we hang out, I don't even want to think about what he'd do. "I can't."

"Come on." He looks at me now. "You can't be working that much? Do you still work nights? I could take you to breakfast."

"No, I *can't*." I look at him and beg him with my eyes to not dig, to not ask why. But it's like he knows everything without me having to say a word.

His mouth forms a tight line. "Has he hurt you?"

I swallow thickly but don't say anything.

"Annie?" His voice is low and angry and I hate that in this moment all I can think about is that I can't remember the last time he called me 'sunshine'. "Did he hurt you?"

I look up at the ceiling, take a deep breath, and then look at Sam. I can't lie to him. For some reason, it's easier to lie to Chiara because she sees Mitch all the time and just like everyone else, she sees the side of him that I fell for. But Sam has never met Mitch.

"I'm my mothers daughter, after all. I know how to pick a winner." Tears prick my eyes but I blink them away.

Sam moves so fast that one second I feel like I'm about to fall apart and the next moment he is wrapping his arms tenderly around me and pulling me against him. "Oh, Annie. You're nothing like your mother."

For the first time in far too long, I feel like I can breathe easily. I feel perfectly safe and okay and normal in his arms and the thought nearly undoes me. I choke out a sob as he pulls me tighter against his chest, one hand holding me to him, and he runs his fingers through my hair with his other hand. We stay like that for a long time, me silently crying and Sam simply holding me.

When my tears run dry, he eases away from me and heads into the kitchen. He returns a moment later with a glass of water. "Drink, or you'll get a headache."

I chug the water as he disappears down the hallway again. When he returns, he's holding my tattered copy of *Emma* that I never got back from him after the bowling alley all those years ago. I nearly start to cry as he sits beside me on the couch, opens the book to the first page, and starts to read.

There are so many words that he and I need to share, like what he's doing here with me and I should tell him about Mitch and everything he's done, but instead, I put my head on his shoulder and listen to his soft candor as he reads aloud my favorite book.

15

SAM

October 2022 - Sam is 28, Annie is 26

I nearly run into an older woman who's calmly walking through the airport in my haste to get a taxi. "Sorry," I yell as I run past, not waiting to hear her response.

I have to get to Annie.

It's been several months since I last saw her, when we stayed up all night and she told me all about her relationship with that vile man and then in the morning she went back to him. I begged her to quit, but she told me she couldn't quit and that she had to ease him out of the relationship again before she could be done for good. I told her that was a crappy reason, but I couldn't convince her before I had to leave again. Because of a contract, I was only in town for three days before I started a backpacking trip all around South America, which is where I was until Noah called me yesterday and told me that I needed to come home.

He needed to be back in Utah, working at his grandma's bookstore and fixing things with Tally. But I needed to come home, to Annie.

Because the boyfriend she couldn't leave hit her—badly. Noah told me to prepare myself and I spent my entire thirteen-hour flight imagining the worst. I haven't been able to eat or sleep. According to Noah, Annie is staying at my apartment and she's officially done with the man I begged her to leave months ago. Thank goodness though.

My taxi driver is chatty, but I can't seem to focus on any of his words. I won't be able to focus on anything until I see Annie until I know that she's okay, that she's alive. I tip extra as I grab my bag from the trunk and sprint up the stairs to my apartment.

I force myself to breathe slowly as I turn the lock on the door. The apartment is dark and quiet and I'm nearly afraid that I won't find her. That my worst fear will be true and she won't be here. I drop my bag before moving into the apartment and stop short when I see her fast asleep on the couch. The right side of her face is black and purple. I fall to my knees and cradle her face in my hands. She stirs but doesn't wake.

"Oh, sunshine," I whisper as I lean my forehead against hers.

Her eyes flutter open. "Sam?"

"I'm here." I move and cradle her against my chest, her arms going around me in an awkward hug as I kneel before her. I'm gentle, unsure of how many unseen injuries she has.

"Thank you for coming," she whispers.

I nod. "Let's get you to bed, it's late."

She nods against my chest and I scoop her up in my arms, bypassing her room and carrying her straight to mine. After she had moved out originally, I'd replaced the twin beds in my room with a queen since Noah had taken her room.

I place her gently on the bed. "I'll be right back," I say as she leans against the pillow and closes her eyes. I hurry to the bathroom and splash cool water on my face. I'd prefer a shower like I generally do after such a long flight, but I don't want to leave her alone for that long. I grab my gray sweats that I keep in the bath-room, slide out of my jeans, and put on something more comfortable. My mind is racing. Noah said that Annie was fine, other than the obvious injuries. She'd told him she'd reported Mitch for what he did and that she had assured him she was fine and so he left.

I send Noah a text, letting him know that I've made it home and I'm with Annie. I want to get back to her, but I know he was waiting for an update. Even though it's late in Utah, he replies immediately.

NOAH

Thanks, man. I wish I could have stayed. But I don't have a ton of time off here at the Book Shop, and if I don't work all my days here, I'll lose the shop. And Tally.

I get it. I'm with her now.

Take care of her for me. She seemed to be doing fine when I left.

I shake my head as I look down at my phone. Noah has always been a protective older brother, always wanting to take care of Annie, but she must have put on one hell of a show for him because he didn't describe the Annie I came home too. And if she had acted the way she is now, he wouldn't have left her alone, not for a minute.

The woman who is lying in my bed? That woman does not seem fine. She seems like a ghost, a shell of who Annie once was. I set my phone on the bathroom counter because I want to give her all of my attention. My hands are shaking as I walk back to my bedroom. Her eyes snap to mine as I pause in the doorway.

"I can sleep on the couch if you're more comfortable..." I say.

She shakes her head. "I don't want to be alone," she whispers, and that's all it takes before I'm crossing the room and crawling onto the other side of the bed. I wrap my arms around her gently as we lie together in silence.

"Can I get you anything for the pain?" I whisper.

She shakes her head again. "Just...hold me?"

"Always."

Her breathing slows long before mine does. My jaw is tight and I try to force thoughts of hurting Mitch out of my mind. I'd really love to go beat up the guy, but I know that would hurt Annie more than it would help this situation. And I just want to be here for her. My arms tighten around her as she settles against me.

While this isn't the first time she's ever slept in my arms, it feels different. I want to hold her and keep her close and safe. I know I won't be able to actually do that. I can't smother Annie. Moonlight shines down on us from in-between the curtains. Annie looks so peaceful while she sleeps.

I'm going to do everything I can for her to feel that peace, always.

No matter what it takes.

I force thoughts of hurting *him* out of my mind and focus on Annie, watching her sleep. I'm just so glad she's okay, at least, kind of okay. I keep my eyes open most of the night, just to reassure myself that she's okay, that she's breathing.

The morning light starts to peek through the curtains before sleep finally claims me.

The other side of the bed is empty when I wake up. The clock on my nightstand tells me it's almost noon.

Something smells delicious though, and when I wander out

into the kitchen, I find Annie at the stove, stirring something in the pan.

"Morning," Annie smiles at me. "I hope it's okay that I'm making your lunch right now. You did sleep through breakfast."

"Sorry," I say. "I didn't sleep much on the plane and it took me a while for my brain to quiet down last night. Did you sleep okay?"

She nods, her cheeks pink. "Better than I have in a while."

That doesn't seem hard to imagine, especially if she was still staying at his house until a few days ago.

"Were you able to get all of your stuff moved in?" I ask as I sit down at the tiny table in the corner of the kitchen.

"Yeah, Noah helped me get all my things while Mitch was working. I don't have a ton of stuff. Just a couple of boxes of books and my suitcase with clothes. And Noah said he'd fill our Mom in about everything, so I don't have to talk to her."

"That's good." Annie and her mom haven't ever had the greatest relationship. I imagine everything will go over better if she hears the news from Noah anyway. I also wonder why Annie doesn't have very many things, she never has. But I don't ask because that seems like a question for another day.

"Are you doing okay?" I ask her.

"Better than last night," she tells me, and I can tell by her tone and body language she's being honest. And truthfully, it's really good to see her in the kitchen. If she wasn't cooking, I'd be worried. "I do have to go to work later though. I couldn't get my shift covered."

"But your face..."

"I know I've got a huge bruise, but I'll only be in the kitchen."

"Will..." the words get lodged in my throat. I can't even ask if he'll be there. Because if he's going to be there, it's bring your friend to work today because there's no way I'm letting Annie go to work alone.

"No," she answers as if she knows what I was going to ask. "He will be out of the state for a couple of weeks. He's meeting with new suppliers for his new restaurant so he won't be around. He left yesterday, I think."

"Are you going to quit?" I know it was her dream to work at Austen's until she could get enough money for her place. But I also know that her grandma left her a nice inheritance so I don't know what would be stopping her.

"Not yet." She looks away from me as she says it. "I can't."

"If you need money..." I start to say but she shakes her head, which is probably a good thing. I've been kind of reckless with my spending for the past two years, and I don't have a ton left in my bank account. Even with money coming in from sponsors and my channel, I've got a team to pay and I don't bring in a significant income these days.

"I don't need money. I just can't quit yet."

"Why not?" I ask her as she sets a steaming plate in front of me.

"I made you my new chicken recipe I've been testing out. Let me know what you think," she says without answering my question.

"Annie," I grab her hand as she starts to walk away. "Why won't you quit?"

I see something like fear flash in her eyes. "I can't. Not yet, but I will soon."

I want to urge her to quit anyway, but something tells me that now is not the time for this conversation. So I wave my white flag, I'm not going to drop this, but I will today. "Okay."

"Okay."

16

ANNIE

April 2023 - Annie is 27, Sam is 28

Sam's been back in New York City for three months and we hang out every single day. I don't know how I feel about it, but I will say that I don't completely hate it. We're friends who live together and nothing more.

I'm the first one awake this morning, after we both fell asleep after watching all three *Hunger Games* movies last night. I stretch, trying to get the kink in my neck out that I got from sleeping on the couch. I look over at Sam, his mouth slightly open and his arm bent above his head. We somehow fell asleep on opposite ends of the couch, and both seemed to sleep mostly comfortably. Well mostly, but I definitely need to try harder to make it back to my bed tonight. I resist the urge to touch him as he takes another sleepy breath, but he looks so peaceful. He's finally stopped looking at me like something that's about to break, and I'm grateful for that. But that shouldn't make me want to touch him.

I sigh as I stand in the middle of the living room, watching him sleep. I wish he'd stop asking me when I'm going to quit my job.

I want to quit.

I want to quit so bad it hurts. Watching him sleep makes me want to quit even more.

We're acting like some sort of couple without all the physical stuff. I make most of our meals, but he always gets me a breakfast bagel after his morning run from the little stand that's around the corner—always a cheesy bagel, light on the cream cheese for me and a cinnamon bagel for him. I need something savory in the morning, and he needs his sugar. We hang out in the evenings on the days I don't work and he stays up late on the nights I do. I don't know how to feel about it—any of it. I turn away from him.

Quitting is what got me—us—here.

Or at least, trying to quit.

I haven't told anyone the full truth of what happened that night with Mitch. The night I ended things for the last time, I also tried to quit my job so I could live peacefully—or at least with more peace—knowing that I wouldn't have to see Mitch several times a week. But it made Mitch angry. He blamed me for all the stress he's been feeling with his new restaurant and told me that if I walked away as his head chef, he'd tell everyone in the food world here in New York not to hire me because I was a bad chef.

He threatened to ruin my reputation. Mitch is well known in the food scene here, so I believe him.

And while Mitch often filled my head with lies, it's hard not to believe him this time since he was yelling and screaming and hitting me as he threatened to ruin me.

I'm out of the relationship, but I can't quit my job. While Mitch has been amicable the past few months, I still get tense every time I see him. Noah would probably kill me if he knew the truth—that I didn't actually report Mitch because I didn't want to make things worse and because I need this job until I can somehow convince Mitch that it will be better for both of us to set me free.

I won't be able to get a new chef position in New York City if I leave Austen's. I don't want to leave the city. That will just mean that Mitch won and he doesn't get to win this one. He doesn't get to take this city I love so much from me.

Sam sighs in his sleep, bringing me back to the present moment. I look at his perfect eyelashes. Why is it that men always seem to get good eyelashes that are long and beautiful while mine are pretty much non-existent unless I wear mascara?

Because I don't want Sam to catch me watching him sleep, I force myself to move and start the day. I'm in the kitchen when he comes up behind me.

"I have to leave next week." Sam's words are quiet like he doesn't want to say them but he has to.

"I know." We haven't explicitly talked about it, but I've heard Sam talking on the phone with his manager and I knew that this day was coming. You can't just leave your job to drop everything and hang out with your best friend's younger sister. I knew he'd have to leave again. Traveling is his job, it's his life. And I won't keep him from that.

"I've got two more short trips and then I can take a break for a while," he tells me. "I've been planning a few months-long break anyway, but now that I took some of those months right now, I can only take a couple at the end of the year."

"Will your subscribers mind?" I ask.

Something shifts on his face. "Well, we'll spread out some of the content like I have been doing, posting only two or three videos a week instead of five or six."

"That's so much content." I mean, I've watched his channel

for years, but I forget that this is his life, making and editing all this content, all the time.

"It's a lot."

"Do you still love it?" I ask. When he first started, you could tell he was excited about traveling and sharing his adventures with the online world. It's funny to me how many people in the comments think they know him from watching his videos, but the videos only tell part of his story. He does have an adventurous side, sure. But that's not the word I would use to describe him.

"Mhm," he answers, but he won't look at me. Why is it so hard for him to tell me the truth?

"I'll be fine while you're gone," I say. "I'll be living here still if that's alright."

"Of course," he replies. "Stay as long as you need."

"Thank you." I move over to him and wrap my arms around him, something that feels almost normal for us. Slowly, as if he had to think about it, he puts his arms around me.

"And you'll quit?" he asks.

I give him a small nod. "I'll try."

17

ANNIE

June 2023 - Annie is 27, Sam is 28

As I leave Austen's, my shoulders relax for the first time all day. I made it through another shift without seeing Mitch. It's late, but I still walk the few blocks home.

I'll try to quit tomorrow. Working for Mitch is killing me, taking a bigger part of me more and more each day. But I haven't figured out how to quit so that he won't completely ruin my career.

I've thought about performing badly, making bad dishes so that he'll fire me. But I don't want to ruin my own reputation. Plus, I don't think I could ever send out a bad dish even if I wanted to get away from Mitch.

Sweat drips down my back as I reach my apartment building.

I'm too tired to think about it now, I don't have to work tomorrow—today I guess—so I'll come up with a better game plan after I've slept. I promised Sam when he left three months ago that I'd try to quit while he was gone, and he'll be back any day now and I still work with and for Mitch. It's something I hate and not a conversation I'm ready to have with Sam about why I'm still working there, because I don't think he'll understand.

When I open the door to our apartment, the cool AC air hits me with sweet relief from the humid night air. I hear the hum of the TV and see the glow of the screen before I see Sam sitting on the couch.

"You're back!" I try to contain the excitement from my voice, but a little slips out. The feeling of relief I had after leaving work grows, but it burns within me and I feel better than I have in weeks. Sam is back.

"Mhm," he says with a grimace.

"What's wrong?" I hurry to him, kneeling in front of him and watch as his face twists in pain as he shifts into a better position. "What happened?"

"Fell," he breathes out, like the word itself pains him.

My stomach squirms. He's done thousands of tricks at this point, but he's always been safe. He's never gotten severely injured, not that I know about anyway. "What happened?"

"Trick went bad," Sam wheezes. "My back."

"We've got to get you to an urgent care," I say, trying to figure out how I'll get him off the couch, down the stairs and into his car and to the urgent care. I'm not super tiny, but he is a lot bigger than me, and he's got a lot more muscle mass and is at least six inches taller than me.

"No." It's the first time Sam's words haven't sounded like he's in pain. "I can't go, they'll tell me I need surgery or some other procedure and I can't afford that. I don't have insurance."

"Don't you make like a million dollars a year?"

He laughs, then winces. "Not that much."

"Why don't you have insurance?" That's stupid. He should have insurance. Especially because of what he does on a day to day basis.

"Too expensive." He closes his eyes. "I spent all my savings. I can't afford surgery. I was just upstate, so the ride back wasn't terrible."

An incredibly ridiculous idea comes to me. "I've got great insurance," I blurt out. The idea is something I've only ever read about in romance novels, but it could work. Because yes, I do occasionally read a romance novel that isn't a classic.

His eyes open and he looks at me for a beat. I can see something brewing underneath the pain. "You didn't quit?"

"I've got great insurance," I repeat, ignoring his question. Somewhere in the back of my mind, I feel like this is a bad idea, one I shouldn't get into, but the words come out anyway. "Let's get married. Then you can get whatever care you need, and if you need it, you can get surgery. You shouldn't just live with this pain in your back."

He looks at me as if I've lost my mind.

Which I probably have. Another thought hits me hard, one that I don't share with Sam. *Maybe if I get married, Mitch will leave me alone, he'll stop holding my career over my head.* I can't say that to Sam though, because then he'll want me to quit so that Mitch stops bothering me—or at least the idea of him will stop bothering me—and Sam still won't be able to get the surgery or whatever care he'll need.

I meet his eyes again, determined to convince him that this plan is foolproof. "We could get married, we could go to the courthouse today and then go to the hospital right after and get you taken care of. My insurance will cover you as soon as we're legally married. It'll be perfect."

He blinks at me. "What?"

"We'll just tell anyone who asks that while you were on your trip we both realized that we should be together, that we've loved each other for so long that it was dumb to not be together any longer." It's not exactly a lie I realize as the words come out.

I love Sam. *I am in love with him.* The realization nearly takes my breath away. I don't know how it happened or what I'm going to do about my feelings, but I love him. I fell in love with my best friend. He's the one I want to call when I have a bad day or even a good day. I look forward to seeing him, and he's the only man I truly feel comfortable around besides my brother —but he doesn't really count, because I'm related to him.

I'm still opposed to the idea of a real marriage and everything that comes with it, especially after what happened with Mitch. But marrying him as his friend so that he can get taken care of and not be in pain anymore? That I can do. I'll worry about my feelings another time. I push them away and watch as Sam takes my proposal in.

"Why would you do that?" he asks, his voice strangled. "You know how I feel about you."

It's my turn to blink at him. I will myself not to blush. Not with my newfound realization that we feel the same way. But now is not the time for feelings, we need to be practical about this. "I'm never going to marry anyone else, Sam. And you can't seem to date a woman long enough to get to the point where you want to propose. I've got great insurance. I can help you. You've done so much for me over the years, let me do this for you." This is logical. And completely delusional, but I won't admit that. I shouldn't marry my best friend—who I also happen to be in love with—simply so he can use my insurance.

But the fact that it could also get Mitch off my back is a huge motivator. And, *I'll be married to Sam.*

He tries to move, then groans in pain. "I'll get you some ice." I hurry to the freezer and come back with a pack of frozen peas. "This is all we have."

"It'll work." Sam groans as he shifts and puts the peas between him and the couch. When his eyes meet mine again, time seems to freeze. Marrying Sam would change everything and both of us know that. But I'd still do it, do this for him. I'd do just about anything to take away the pain he's in. Including becoming his wife, even if I always promised myself I wouldn't be anyone's wife. I swallow thickly as I watch his eyes flicker to my lips for a heartbeat and then search my eyes again.

"Marry me," I say. "For the insurance."

But we both know it's not just for the insurance. I wonder who will be the first to break and tell the truth. My guess is Sam, because I don't plan to ever tell him the whole truth.

"Yes, I'll marry you, sunshine." His voice is low.

I try to focus on something else. "You must be in a lot of pain, can I get you anything that will help so you can get some sleep?"

His next look chills me to the bone. "I've been in worse pain, this is nothing. Get some sleep, sunshine. We're getting married today."

My heart squeezes in my chest with guilt but I nod and move away from him. "Just holler if you need anything."

He nods, but we both know he won't. Even though we're getting married some time today, he's not exactly happy about it. This isn't how he wanted this to happen, but he'll do it anyway. Even if it means one or both of us ending up with a broken heart.

It takes me another hour for my mind to stop whirling and to fall into a fitful sleep. When I wake up, I'm getting married.

Something I never planned on happening. Something I never expected.

I don't think I'll mind marrying Sam. It's the last thought I have before I fall asleep.

When I get up a few hours later, I shower and put on a simple yellow sundress and head out to the kitchen only to find Sam eating a bowl of cereal at the kitchen island.

"I could have made you breakfast," I say as I pull out my frozen spinach and strawberries to put in my usual morning smoothie.

"It's okay," he answers, his voice soft and he won't look at me. "You're already marrying me today, I can't exactly ask you to do anything else."

I swallow thickly. "It was my idea to get married, and I'm happy to do it. So don't feel like you can't ask me for help."

He nods and walks stiffly around the counter to put his bowl in the sink. "We don't have to get married, I'll set up a GoFundMe or something and I'm sure I can pay for any of the medical help I need if I do that."

"Sam." I walk up to him—but don't touch him—as I search his eyes. "I want to do this."

I wait for him to ask why, ready to tell him the truth. Because he deserves to know the truth, but I can't seem to bring myself to say the words. How does one tell the person they love that they love them without completely blurting it and sounding like a lunatic? But he doesn't ask, he simply looks down at me with a face that I can't read. I've never been able to not read Sam and know what he's thinking or feeling, but this morning I don't know and it makes me nervous.

"Only if you're sure, Annie," he finally says. "I'll only do this if you're sure you want to marry me. For insurance." He adds the last part like he knows the truth, like he knows how I really feel about him but that I'm too afraid to admit it.

Three little words are on the tip of my tongue, but instead I say, "I'm sure."

He nods once. "Give me about a half hour to get ready, then we'll go." He walks slowly out of the kitchen.

"Do you need help changing?" I ask, turning red down to my toes at the thought of having to help him change, of taking off his clothes.

He looks back at me, taking in my crimson skin and a smirk slides onto his face, which makes me go warm all over. "Nah, I'll be fine. Plus, like you said last night, I don't think this will be that type of marriage."

It's as if a bucket of ice water was dumped on me. Before I regain enough composure to reply, he turns and heads into his bedroom, closing the door with a gentle click.

I'm wiping down the kitchen counters when he returns. "Do you have your birth certificate?"

"I grabbed all my important documents. They're in the folder." I nod to the manila folder sitting on the edge of the counter.

He grabs the folder and adds his own documents to it, like we're already sharing space and becoming one or whatever it is married couples do. This is really about to happen.

We take the subway and Sam stands the entire ride because he says that sitting hurts too much. I can tell he's in pain as we climb the stairs of the courthouse, but when I ask him about it, he tells me he's fine.

"Ready?" Sam asks before we go in.

"Ready," I say, because what else am I supposed to say? I'm the one who suggested we do this in the first place. He slides my hand into his as we walk through the doors of the courthouse.

I look at him in surprise.

"They aren't going to believe us if we aren't even touching," he whispers as we follow the signs to where we need to go to get a marriage certificate. I am fairly certain that the people here don't care at all whether we're holding hands or not, but I don't let go. I ignore the pulse of electricity that hums through my body at our interconnected hands. This doesn't mean anything,

I try to tell my body. This is a purely platonic marriage. I have to remember that.

"We're here to get a marriage license and get married today." Sam grins at the older woman behind the desk.

She doesn't even look up. "First door on your left, they'll get you all sorted."

Sam leads us into the next room where we're given all the paperwork we need to get our marriage license. They make copies of all our legal documents then lead us to a waiting area after giving us the document.

"There are no scheduled weddings today," a man in a gray suit informs us. "So I expect they'll get you in soon. Did you bring your own witnesses?"

Sam leans close to me and leaves a feather light touch with his lips against my cheek. It's a whisper of a kiss and I have to ignore the sudden urge to pull him in and kiss him for real. I can't let my actual feelings get involved in this marriage. That would be disastrous for both of us. "We didn't think that far ahead," Sam tells the man, his eyes never leaving me.

"That's fine. We have people who can assist. Congratulations."

"Thanks," Sam murmurs. He's looking at me like he's really in love with me and can show it for the first time ever. Like we're so in love that we had to come to the courthouse today because waiting any longer would have been unbearable.

The man returns to his desk and Sam straightens himself, as if the way he was just looking at me didn't even happen.

"You'd be good at fake dating," I whisper.

He looks at me out of the corner of his eye.

"You're acting like you're in love with me," I say the words, but we both know that Sam isn't acting. He's never acted when it came to me, that's why we didn't talk much while I was with Mitch, it hurt too much. It's also why I have to put on the best performance of my life. Feelings complicate everything. *My feelings will complicate everything.*

"Who's to say that I'm not?" He sighs and looks down at the floor. Before I can respond, tell him that maybe this is a bad idea and I don't actually want to break his heart when all of this is over, the judge appears and invites us to follow him. There are two older women—probably in their eighties—who are going to be our witnesses. One of them smiles at us as we take our places. I glance away, shifting under their gazes.

His eyes capture mine and he gives me an encouraging smile. I can do this. I *want* to do this.

I barely focus on what the judge is saying throughout the ceremony. Sam watches me carefully the entire time, my hands in his.

"Do you Annie Mae Jones take Sam Holland to be your husband?" The judge asks me. This is it.

"Yes," I look at Sam, "I do."

Sam swallows as he watches me and the judge asks him if he'll take me to be his wife. "I do." Sam's voice is low and gravely.

I lick my lips and Sam watches every movement. I never imagined any type of wedding for myself, but I think if I had imagined it, it would have been like this, no frills and fanfare. Just me and Sam.

"Congratulations," the judge says, breaking my thoughts. "Mary will help you finish up the paperwork. You may now kiss the bride to end the ceremony."

18

———

SAM

June 2023 - Annie is 27, Sam is 28

Annie doesn't blink as she looks at me and I'm not sure what she's thinking. It's not like she and I haven't kissed before, we've kissed in the past. But this feels different because it is different. This will be our first kiss as husband and wife.

I swallow thickly as I lean in close to her and Annie shivers when my lips brush her ear. "We don't have to kiss if you don't want to."

"It's fine," she says, her voice a little bit breathless. Maybe she isn't as unaffected by all of this as she lets on. Maybe, she's not been completely truthful about her feelings. But I don't let myself cling to that hope, I need to remind myself exactly why she's marrying me and not expect anything more. I can't let myself want anything more or else I'll just be setting myself up for heartbreak.

I move slightly and Annie turns to me, our noses brush. She lets out a nervous laugh.

My heart thunders in my chest. Is she nervous because she has feelings for me?

The judge has already moved away, but the witnesses still have their eyes on us. Two older women who seem to be giddy about the fact that they just got to watch someone get married. I focus on Annie's pink lips—lips I've dreamed about kissing again a million times, but never like this. Never as my wife. I never let myself fall into that daydream because it always hurt too much.

I get to kiss the love of my life—my wife—today, I think as I pull Annie toward me. I'm not about to screw this up or skip out on the chance to do that.

I curl a hand around her neck as our noses brush again. Her eyes flutter closed and I close mine as I press my lips against hers.

Her hands fist my T-shirt as our lips come together and I pull her closer. She relaxes into our kiss, and I kiss her deeply. I may not ever get this chance again, and we may as well enjoy it in this moment. It feels so perfect to have her in my arms, to be kissing her like this. Everything about this feels right and normal. Like everything has finally fallen into place. Alarm bells sound in my head, reminding me of all the reasons why this is a bad idea—why I can't actually kiss her like this. They give me a moment of clarity and I pull away before I let myself fall too hard, but I think it's too late for that.

She is breathing just as hard as I am as we stare at each other. Her cheeks turn crimson as one of the witnesses claps and she turns away from me. I hold her hand as we walk back to the reception area where we have to sign more paperwork.

She refuses to look at me while we sign the rest of the paperwork and a woman tells us our marriage certificate will be sent to us in the mail in the next few days. But it's official, we're married.

"Annie," I say as hot June air hits us when we exit the courthouse.

She looks up at me. "I'll talk to HR tonight and get the

paperwork moving so you can be on my insurance. We can go to the doctor tomorrow."

I nod, jaw tight. The pain in my back that I so conveniently forgot during the ceremony comes rushing back. So this how it's going to be then, no eye contact after we just became husband and wife. Purely business. I should have expected it, but her avoidance still stings.

"I've got work tonight, so I need to get ready," she tells me.

I grit my teeth. I know she's lying, she doesn't work on Tuesdays. She hasn't in months. "Okay," I say and we walk the rest of the way to our apartment in silence.

She disappears into her room as I ease myself onto the couch. My back hurts, but it doesn't hurt as much as the pain in my heart. I feel as though I just made the worst mistake I could have possibly made. I married my best friend, the woman I've loved for over ten years and she doesn't actually want to be married to me. She's only doing this so I can be out of physical pain. But none of the physical pain I feel even matters if she won't even look at me.

She murmurs a quick goodbye before leaving the apartment and I stare at the ceiling in agonizing silence. Annie Jones is my wife, something I never thought would happen. And it feels worse than I ever expected it to.

The next three weeks pass by in a blur. My surgery is scheduled for tomorrow now that I've been added to Annie's insurance. I am still making money from my videos on YouTube, but I made a short video, explaining there wouldn't be videos for awhile because of my surgery and it's incredible how angry people are. How these strangers on the internet feel like they are entitled to new content from me even while I'll be recovering from surgery.

I mentioned the comments to Annie and she made me delete the app from my phone so I would stop reading them. It makes me wonder if I should simply quit for good. I've had the thought—just a passing one—a couple of times in the past couple of months, and now that I'm hurt and having to have surgery, it makes me want to stop even more.

I'm a married man now, and while that may not mean much to Annie, it means something to me. And the lifestyle I've been living since I graduated high school just isn't going to work for me anymore. It's not going to work for us anymore—even if the us part is only inside my head.

"You ready for tomorrow?" Annie asks me as she sits on the couch next to me, careful not to actually touch me. Things have slowly been getting back to normal between us and I'm thankful. It's still awkward in that she's stiff and refuses to touch me even accidentally, but we're talking like we used to.

"I think so," I say truthfully. I'm ready to be out of so much pain, but I know that physical therapy and all my recovery isn't going to be a walk in the park either. "I can still call Noah or one of my sisters to help with recovery and everything."

She shakes her head. "It's fine, Sam. I can do it. I went down to part-time hours, with full benefits still because of how long I've been working at Austen's. Plus this way, I have less of a chance of running into him."

Now, we both avoid saying *his* name. It never used to be like that, but that's how I knew it was the last time she'd leave him when I came back a few months ago. She never calls him by name.

"Is he still giving you trouble?" I ask and her mouth forms a thin line.

"I haven't seen him in months, but I'm just waiting for the fallout when he finds out I've married you."

"How will he know?" I ask.

"He's a control freak. He'll find out if he notices that I'm paying more for insurance," she says, and I reach out and squeeze her hand, letting her know that I'm here for her. She doesn't pull away.

"I'm sorry," I say, wishing I could do something.

"Why?" She looks at me. "You've been a better man with an injured back the past three weeks than he's ever been in all the time I dated him."

I swallow thickly, unsure of how to respond.

She reaches for the remote and turns on an old episode of *Hell's Kitchen*. "I'm sure your surgery will be fine," Annie says out of nowhere a moment later and I realize the words aren't to calm *me* down. I'm not worried about the surgery. I bite back my grin, because if she's worried, it means she cares. "The surgeon seems quite capable and he said it would be fine."

He did say the surgery would help with the pain, and I guess that's all that really matters.

19

———

ANNIE

June - August 2023

"Could you explain the surgery to me again?" I ask the surgeon one last time. Sam is already getting prepped for surgery and I follow the surgeon out into the hallway. "Of course." His doctor gives me a smile as if he's seen this before—a concerned wife wanting to know all about what's going to happen to her husband. I can't explain why I feel so nervous. The doctor assured Sam that everything was going to be fine, but still, I know that Sam was hiking when he hurt his back and that he was about to rock climb a cliffside when he slipped and landed ten feet down on his back.

I want to hear about it again. "Sam has a herniated disk, which is what is causing him a lot of pain. I'll be doing a nucleoplasty which simply means I put a needle into the disk and then a laser does the work of vaporizing the tissue and relieving pressure on the nerves."

"And it's a good solution?" I ask again.

The doctor nods. "His herniated disk is mild, so this surgery will be minimally invasive and should help with the pain. He'll be back to his normal activities in the next eight to twelve weeks, with some normal activity in three to six weeks. If all goes well, he won't have to have any other surgeries."

"Thank you, Doctor Miller," I say and head back into Sam's room.

He smiles when he sees me.

"You ready to be out of pain?" I ask.

"Definitely. Can you believe they don't even completely put me out for the surgery? I mean, I'll be sleepy and get numbed where they stick the needle in, but I get to go home today."

The nurse and doctor both mentioned this and I still can't believe that you can have back surgery and be home later that day.

"I'll be here when you get back," I tell him. I'm feeling too many feelings right now and I'm not ready to share them. I can stick with the simple things, the things that are happening right in front of me. Like his surgery.

But I'm not about to talk about how it all makes me feel. I can't even think about it. I haven't thought about the realization I had before we got married—the fact that I love him—and I definitely haven't thought about our kiss after the ceremony.

And by definitely haven't I mean it's less than a thousand times. Probably.

He gives me a wry grin, as if he knows that I'm thinking about our kiss. "See you later, sunshine," he calls as they wheel him out of the room.

"How are you feeling?" I ask him for what feels like the millionth time in the past three weeks. His surgery went well and he seems to be doing okay, like right now he's rearranging his bookshelf, which doesn't seem like something he should be doing so soon after having surgery.

"I'm fine," he answers without looking at me.

"I could organize your books for you," I offer. "I could even bring out some of mine." The words slip out. As if my brain wants us to start cohabitating in a way that is more like the newlyweds we are than the roommates we've always been.

He looks up at me with a sly grin, the same one he gave me right before his surgery. "You should bring out some of your books, I've seen your shelf, it's overflowing. There's plenty of space on this one."

I shouldn't have said anything. But he is looking at me now as if he's waiting for me to back down, as if he's waiting for me to admit my bluff or tell the truth. Sighing, I head down the hall to my room and scan my bookshelf.

Books are such a personal thing, and sharing them in the same space as someone else when I haven't ever done that feels terrifying. I select a few of my well worn favorites and bring them out to the living room.

"Here." I set them down by one of his piles.

He snorts. "That's it? You afraid of what it means if our books are on the same shelf?"

"No." I fold my arms defensively. "I just don't want to take up too much of your space."

I watch as he licks his lips before looking up at me from his seat on the ground. "Alright," he says, "we can go with that. For now."

I take a startled step back. Is he flirting with me? "Alright," I say back as naturally as possible, but my skin is covered in goosebumps as I turn away. Could he and I actually make this marriage thing work? Do I even want it to work?

It's nearly dark when I get home from work, but Sam looks up at me from sitting on the couch when I walk into the apartment.

"How was work?" he asks as I drop my bag and keys and slip off my shoes.

"Good," I say, but it's not true. Not anymore. Being a chef at Austen's hasn't been bringing me the same joy it used to. All it does is bring me stress and make me feel tense. But I can't tell Sam that, because then he'll convince me that I need to quit—because I do—and I don't know what I'll do if I do end up quitting. I don't know how to take the next step in my life without more planning. "How was your day?"

He shrugs, and then lifts a take-out carton, "I got Indian food from that place down the street that you like."

I touch my hand to my chest. "You know the way to my heart."

He smiles at that as I sit down beside him on the couch. This is how it's been for the past two weeks. It's almost like we're tip-toeing around each other because we don't know how to act now that we're married. His back doesn't hurt him at all these days, which means his surgery worked. It's only been six weeks since his surgery, but he seems to be recovering well.

He also hasn't gone back to work yet and when I asked about it a few days ago, he said he was just going to wait the twelve weeks that the doctor told him he should take it pretty easy—meaning no tricks—before traveling again.

"So, what did you do all day?" I ask at the same time he says, "would you want to come on a trip with me sometime?"

I blink at him slowly and feel my face grow warm as he watches me. I glance away and take a bite of the spicy tikka masala before answering. "I'm not really into some of the adventures you go on."

"I know," he says, "I was just thinking it could be fun. I

could take you to some of my favorite places in Europe or we could go somewhere by the ocean that has a resort and a pool."

I lick my lips and look at him, trying not to picture the romantic getaway he didn't even describe. At least, not directly. "That would be fun."

That would be fun? *That would be fun?* That's all I can say? I actually agreed to it? He smiles again.

"I'll start planning something, then."

"Sam?" I ask and he shifts slightly so his knee brushes against mine. "What is this, what are we?"

This is not the conversation I planned on having today, but it feels like something we should talk about. I want to ask if he's felt the shift between us. I want to tell him that I love him, that I've loved him for a long time and that I didn't marry him only so he could use my insurance, but I'm too afraid to say the words.

He meets my eyes. "What do you mean?"

"Us. Like, what is this between us?"

I watch his Adam's apple bob as he swallows. "You and me, Annie, that's who we are. And what's between us? I'm not really sure at this point, but I'd like to find out."

"Yeah?" I ask.

"Yes." His phone rings before I can reply. "It's Noah, I should take this."

I nod, because he should. We still haven't told Noah that we got married. Partly because I wasn't ever intending to stay married to Sam, but now I don't know what's going to happen. But if we do decide to stay together, and try for real, we'll have to figure out a way to tell Noah.

20

ANNIE

October 2023 - Annie is 27, Sam is 29

I pace back and forth in our apartment, glancing at the front door every single minute, hoping that Sam doesn't burst in at any moment. I know he's at a meeting with his team, so he probably won't be back anytime soon, but I need to tell Emily my news. I've barely been able to hear a word she's said about her latest pregnancy. I have to tell her my news before I burst. She's my best friend, my longest friend, she needs to know.

She's talking about how she'll need to buy more baby onesies when I finally interrupt her. "Emily, I'm married."

There's a stunned silence on the other end of the line.

"Um, you're going to have to repeat that, because I could have sworn you just said that you're married and the Annie Jones I know has been promising anyone and everyone for all her life that marriage was one thing she was never going to do."

I walk into my bedroom and sink down onto the bed. Sam and I might be married, but things are the same as they were before we got married, except all of the awkwardness that came after we went to city hall is gone.

"I married Sam three months ago," I tell my childhood best friend and have to pull the phone away from my ear as she starts squealing. We may not talk all the time, but Emily is still the person I want to tell everything to. I can't believe I waited this long to tell her about what I did.

"Finally! Tell me all the things. What's it like being married? How's the sex? I bet he's good…"

"Emily!" I shriek to cut her off. "It's not that kind of marriage."

"What do you mean it's not that kind of marriage? That man is gorgeous."

"He needed back surgery. I have great insurance. We both knew I'd never marry anyone else so it was the perfect solution." I tell her the facts, I can stick with the facts, but I will not tell her about how much I wish it was a real marriage but how I'm too afraid of what will happen if I let Sam in on that little fact.

"Annie, you've been in love with him for years. Are you sure this is a good idea?"

I ignore Emily's words. "Too late for that now."

"Sweetie," Emily says in her motherly voice. "I don't want to see you get hurt. Have you told him how you feel?"

I sigh. "No."

"You should tell him. Imagine what your life could be like if you told him. The man adores you." Emily sighs as if she's in love with the idea of me and Sam being happily married and in love.

"Not gonna happen," I say.

"But you do love him still, right?" Emily was the one I called when Sam first got a girlfriend after we moved out to New York. The first time I realized he was seriously trying to get over me and not just date around. I poured out my heart to her and she told me I was being an idiot, that I should have just told him the truth instead of hiding from my feelings. It's been years and every now and then she bugs me about it, saying I should just get everything out in the open, but I don't want to ruin my friendship with Sam.

Plus, I hate how much I regret hiding from my feelings, because hiding from my feelings for Sam led to me dating Mitch. But I still can't tell him.

"Yes. I'm not ready." I don't know if I'll ever be ready to give my heart to another person the way I did with Mitch, even if that person is Sam.

"You'll be ready someday," she says as if her words settle the matter. "I just hope Sam is still around when you finally get there. But you really married him? And he had to have back surgery? I feel like I missed an entire chapter of your life. Tell me everything."

So I do, tell her everything. I just leave out all the feelings but Emily knows me better than that. We both know what I'm not saying.

"I can't believe you got married without me!" She says after a few minutes of silence.

Guilt squeezes in my chest. "I know, I'm sorry. It just kind of happened really fast. He needed insurance so I suggested we go get married later that day."

"Well," she says. "If you two decide to make it official official, I'm going to throw you a huge party. You'll have to come to the middle of nowhere Nebraska so I can throw you a party, because I can't travel, but we're going to make it happen."

"You really think I should tell him." It's not a question.

"Of course I think you should tell him," she tells me. "I think you're being stupid by not telling him."

"Gee thanks."

"Annie, you know what I mean," she says.

"I mean, I guess." I bite my lip. "But what if it ruins everything?"

"But what if it makes everything magical? What if the two of you get a fairytale romance, don't you want that?" Emily married a guy we went to high school with straight out of college. She's happy in her life as a wife and mother, but I don't know if I'm ready for that.

"I don't know."

"Don't you want Sam?"

My cheeks burn. "What do you mean?"

"I mean," Emily says, "that you've loved that man for a long time. You've lived with him for just as long. You've kissed him, and if I recall you once told me that it was the best kiss in your entire life. So what I mean is exactly what I said, don't you want Sam?"

I think of his soft hands on my cheeks and neck as he kissed me at our wedding ceremony. My toes curl. I'd love to kiss him again. "Well, yes."

Emily laughs, a sound that breaks something open in me.

"You should tell him. Or just kiss him and see what happens."

"Gah."

"What?" she asks and I hear a child in the background, which means our phone call is about to end.

"Nothing, you just gave me a lot to think about."

"Don't think, just do."

"We'll see." I have to work later, so it's not like Sam and I can have any sort of conversation until tomorrow anyway. He'll probably be asleep by the time I get home.

"I've gotta go," Emily starts.

"I know, I heard your kid," I say with a smile. Emily is a great mom. If I ever decide to have kids someday, I hope I can be like her.

"He's been very snuggly lately," she tells me. "I think he knows there's about to be a new baby."

"Well, enjoy your snuggles."

"You too," she says with a voice that I know all too well. She's planning something.

"No texting Sam and meddling." I have to stop her before she does something drastic. I can handle this. I will tell Sam my feelings, sometime.

"What? I would never."

"Ha. Just please don't say anything yet. I'll talk to him soon," I tell her, already formulating how we can have a casual but also serious conversation tomorrow. I'm ready to take things to the next level. To actually be a couple. If Sam is ready for that.

"Okay..." Emily says and I hear a little voice over the phone. "I have to go, but if you don't say anything soon, I will start to meddle."

"You wouldn't dare," I say, but I'm smiling. Grateful to have a friend who cares so much about me and my happiness.

"Go get your man."

21

———

SAM

End of December 2023 - sam is 29, Annie is 27

As soon as I enter our apartment, I know something is wrong. Our Christmas tree twinkles in the corner, since we haven't taken it down yet. I was planning to ring in the new year alone. Annie had to go into work this afternoon, since she was working on the new menu. She should still be there, since she has a shift tonight. I wasn't planning to see her today, since I knew my meeting with my team would go long as we went over the logistics of me stepping back from making so many videos and traveling all the time. I also have a few errands to run, but I didn't rush, because I knew I'd be staying up to wait for Annie anyway. But the shower is running even though the apartment is completely dark. I drop my keys and the groceries I bought on my way home from physical therapy onto the counter.

I knock on the bathroom door. "Annie?"

When she doesn't reply, I twist the knob, every nerve in my body is telling me that something is wrong and I prepare myself to find her black and blue like I did a year ago. Instead, I find Annie sitting in the bathtub fully clothed. The water from the shower is pelting her back and she has her arms wrapped around her legs. I reach in and pull my hand back in shock—the water beating down on her is ice cold. I turn the shower off.

"Annie, what happened?" Her eyes are glassy as she looks up at me and her lips are turning blue. "We've got to get you into dry clothes and get you warm, can you stand?"

Annie doesn't respond, she just leans against the wall and closes her eyes as if the thought of moving is too much work. Terror rips through me. "Annie!" I shout and she blinks her eyes open. "I'm going to get you out of the tub and I have to change your clothes because you're soaked and freezing, is that okay?"

"Yeah," Annie whispers before closing her eyes again. I pull her out of the tub and carry her to my room. Carefully, I set her on my bed and hurry to her closet, grabbing a pair of sweats and a sweatshirt that I realize she must have taken from my closet because it's mine. I grab some underwear from her top drawer and hurry back to her. She's still in her chef's jacket. I make quick work unbuttoning in and slowly slide it off. Her undershirt is sticking to her skin.

"Arms up, love," I whisper and while Annie's eyes still look out of focus, like she's not completely here with me, she raises her arms. The undershirt is harder to remove than the chef's jacket because it's sticking to her skin but I get it off. Now she's in her slacks and a light pink bra. "I'm going to take off your bra now," I tell her softly. "But I promise I won't look."

Annie merely nods as my fingers find the bra hooks and I unhook them. I keep my eyes on her face as the fabric slips off her body and I wrap the towel around her shoulders to quickly dry her off before pulling on my hoodie without glancing at her chest.

"Time for your pants," I say. Annie's shaking now and I need to get her under the covers as soon as possible. "Lift your hips for me?" She falls back onto the bed and raises her hips. I slide her pants down. Her underwear is soaked and freezing but I don't know if I can strip her bare in this condition.

"You're thinking too much, help me change," Annie says softly. "I'm so cold, Sam. I can't do it myself."

I nod once, even though she can't see me and snap my eyes shut as I slide her underwear off her body. Somehow, she helps me dry off her legs and I only look at her ankles to get her sweats on then close my eyes again as I pull them up the rest of the way. Once Annie is fully clothed and her wet clothes are on the floor, I throw back the covers and pull her into my arms and wrap the blankets around us like a cocoon.

"I didn't look," I tell her as she trembles with cold against me.

"You could have," she says so quietly I almost don't hear her. "I'm your wife after all."

My mouth goes dry at her words, surely she's not aware of what she just said. But even if she was, it doesn't matter. The only thing that matters is getting her warm. I take her hands, which are like icicles, and put them in mine and I pull her back against my chest.

"Time to warm up, sunshine."

"Mmm," is all Annie says in response and then we lie together in silence.

When I wake up a few hours later, Annie is still in my arms, but now we're facing each other and she's already looking at me.

"Hi," she says quietly.

"Hi," I say as I rub her back. "Want to talk about what happened?"

Annie shakes her head. "Not really, but I probably should."

"Are you okay?" I ask as I pull her to me, her head on my chest.

"Not really."

When Annie moves her face again, our noses brush but she doesn't pull away. "I ran into him. I mean, I knew it would happen at some point, but it happened today."

I simply watch her eyes and try to keep the rage I feel hidden. Annie already went through the ringer today with whatever happened, I'm not about to make it worse just because whenever he comes up my blood boils.

"It was fine at first, I was just prepping the kitchen for tonight's service when he asked if he could talk to me in his office alone."

"You don't have to tell me everything if you don't want to," I tell her, I don't want to make her re-live it if she doesn't want to.

Annie closes her eyes and takes a deep breath before opening them again and that's when I see the tears. "I can't even repeat what he said. It was so awful. But, I think some of what he said might actually be true."

"Oh, no, sunshine." I pull Annie closer to me and our legs tangle together as she grips my shirt and cries into it. I run my fingers through her hair. "I can promise that whatever he said wasn't true. He doesn't know you. He only cares about himself, and he wants to take back whatever power he thinks he can get and that's why he said what he did."

When Annie stops crying, she looks up at me, her eyes clearer than they've been in weeks. "Kiss me, Sam."

My jaw drops open in shock. "Are you sure?" I don't want her to kiss me simply because she wants to forget about her bad day. I don't even know if I should kiss her because of what she went through today. Do you kiss someone when they're in a vulnerable state even if they ask you?

"I've been trying to work up the courage to ask you for

weeks," she says, not taking her eyes off of mine and I see a faint blush crawl up her cheeks. "I had a whole conversation planned...but that will have to wait. Right now I feel warm and safe in your arms. So will you kiss me?"

I brush her hair out of her face and take in her eyes—that somehow seem brighter after she's cried—and all the freckles that cover her nose and down to her soft pink lips. The same lips that drive me crazy most nights in my sleep. But I don't know if I can do it. I don't want to cause her any more heartache

"Any day now, Sam," she says with a laugh and moves one of her hands to my face. I could cry in relief at how warm they are.

"I was so scared," I tell her. "When I got home and found you in the shower."

"I'm sorry," she says.

"Don't be sorry, I just... I want to be here for you, okay?"

"Okay."

"And I don't want to push you into doing something with me just because you've had a bad day."

Annie leans forward so our noses brush. She runs one of her hands through my hair. "Don't you see it Sam? How I feel about you? Maybe now isn't the time to talk about it, but we will need to have that conversation. But right now? Right now I want to kiss you. Or you to kiss me."

I want to cradle her in my arms and keep her safe from everything. Does she mean what I think she means? Does she love me? I want to ask, but she's said we can talk later, and I'll just have to trust that. "Alright, sunshine."

She grins at me.

I close the remaining distance between us, and just like our kisses in the past, it feels like I've come home. Annie has always been my home, my North Star. She's my everything and I want to show her just exactly what she means to me. So I kiss her tenderly, one hand on her hip and the other in her hair. Holding her steady as I kiss her in a way that I hope shows just how much I love her.

Annie's kiss turns needy as she tries to pull herself closer to me. I've got a lot of self-control but not that much.

I pull back from her every so slightly. "Slow down, sunshine."

She blinks up at me as if she can't believe that she lost control of herself just a little.

"I'll kiss you all night, we've got plenty of time."

And that's exactly what I do.

22

ANNIE

January 2024

Peace. All I feel is peace. Sam's heavy arm is wrapped around my waist, pinning me to him, not that I want to move out of his warm embrace. But I've been mostly awake for the past hour and my stomach has been grumbling for most of it.

"Sam?" I ask, not wanting to pop the bubble we've been in for the past two days. We've spent most of them in bed, talking, laughing, and kissing. Lots and lots of kissing.

"Mhm?" he murmurs against my shoulder.

"I'm starving."

He laughs and his entire body shakes mine. "I was having a good dream," he tells me as he slips out of the bed and pulls on a shirt. "Want a bagel?"

"Yes please." I sit up and his shirt that I've been wearing slips further off my shoulder. His eyes follow the movement.

"But I'm going to stay here, okay?"

"I'll be back in a few." He grabs his keys and his wallet and I sigh, leaning back in the bed. I reach for my phone for the first time in two days.

I have a dozen missed calls from Chiara and other co-workers and a handful from Austen's. I groan, but I've got to get this over with. I open Chiara's text thread.

Chiara: Are you okay? You went in to meet with Mitch and then you left and Mitch left and he looked furious.

Chiara: Is everything alright? You've missed another shift and that's not like you.

Chiara: I asked Mitch what was going on and he told me and the other staff that because of a family matter, you won't be returning to Austen's. What happened!?

I text her back: Mitch isn't telling you the truth. Well, I'm not coming back to Austen's, but he's the reason why.

Chiara texts back almost seconds later.: YOU'RE ALIVE! I was about to send out a search party. He's the reason your face was bruised, isn't he?

Chiara and I never talked about what Mitch did to me, but it turns out she's a better friend than I gave her credit for.

Me: Yes. Our history is long and complicated, but it's done. I'm finally free.

My hands shake as I type the words that I so desperately want to believe, but I don't yet. Maybe if I say them enough, they will feel true.

Chiara: I'm proud of you, but you should know that I overheard Mitch talking on the phone to some food critic this morning. He's trying to ruin you. But I'll back you up. I'm putting in my letter of resignation today.

I drop my phone as I read Chiara's words. He's really doing it. Mitch is making good on his threat to make it impossible for me to get a job here. In this place that I love. I don't respond, instead I put my phone on my nightstand.

Can I stay here in New York? Is it even worth it to stay? Or should I go? Mitch is really going to ruin me more than he already has.

I have to take several deep breaths to not throw up.

I'm pacing the kitchen when Sam returns with breakfast.

"What's wrong?" he asks, concern lacing his features. I don't want to dump this on him. Sam, who's too good for this world. For me. I can't ruin him with all the anxieties in my head and the fear I have from the past.

"I have to go," I tell him.

"Huh?" He sets the bagels on the counter. "What are you talking about?"

This is exactly why I shouldn't have told him or let him kiss me. I shouldn't have even implied that I feel the same way as him, because now I'll want him to come with me.

"I have to leave New York," I tell him. I've been thinking about it for the past fifteen minutes since Chiara's texts. This is what I need to do. "I need a new start."

"Okay, let's get packed then." Sam says.

I look up at him sadly. "You should stay."

His face falls.

"I need to do this alone."

"You don't have to run, Annie. We can slow down and—" he starts but I shake my head.

"This isn't about you or me. The past couple of days have been incredible." I walk over to him and squeeze his hand, then take a step back. I shouldn't make this harder than it's already going to be. "They've been perfect. But I can't stay in the city and I can't ask you to come with me."

"I'm your husband, Annie. I'd follow you anywhere."

"But you shouldn't have to. You've made a life here. You need to travel again for your channel, your subscribers have been waiting for a new video. You should go travel and...and when I'm ready you can come with me."

"Annie." He closes the distance between us as his voice breaks. "Don't do this. You don't have to be tough and deal with whatever you're dealing with all on your own. I'm here."

I hold back a sob. I want him to come with me, but I can't ask him to do that. I don't even know where I'm going to go. All I know is that I think I need some space, and maybe a therapist. And I need to go to a place where I won't run into Mitch ever again.

"I need to do this myself," I say, pulling myself from his arms. "I'm sorry."

He looks heartbroken, but he nods. "If that's what you think is best."

"I do, I'm sorry," I say again.

"Don't be sorry," Sam says softly, and I wish he was angry instead. I wish he was yelling, but he's just his usual loving self. "Just do what you need to do and I'll be ready for you when you're ready."

"You shouldn't let me stop you from living your life, from dating other women."

He cringes, as if the thought of dating other women pains him. When his eyes meet mine, all I see is love and adoration—love and adoration that I don't deserve. "You are my life, sunshine."

I turn away before he can see the tears in my eyes. I hurry to my room and an hour later, I'm pulling my suitcase behind me and he is nowhere to be found. I glance around the apartment one last time. So many firsts happened here, and now it's time to leave.

PART TWO
COLORADO

23

ANNIE

January 2024

I end up booking a flight to Colorado after leaving the apartment. I don't want to go home, but I feel like maybe the mountains will help me. People like nature, right? That's where they go to get help and I need help.

After I land, I book an Uber and I pick Estes Park as my destination instead of Kersey. There is nothing waiting for me in my hometown, not anymore, and maybe the small, touristy mountain town is exactly what I need. I hope it'll be what I need, since I just left my husband in New York. My husband. I squeeze my eyes shut and picture Sam's perfect face. His soft jaw that's always been kind of a baby face—like he never grew out of it after high school—which is probably why he always has a beard these days. I imagine him looking at me, a look that makes me feel so loved and adored. My fingers itch and I want to text him, tell him that I'm okay, but I can't, not yet. I left him and while I know it was the right choice, I need space and to figure out what is happening inside my brain, it still sucks.

I'm starting over again, and for the first time in the past ten years, he isn't here to do this with me. Some things, you have to do on your own. My Uber picks me up and I slip my headphones into my ears and start playing 1989, the one album that always seems to calm me down. I've never really been a pop person, but if Taylor Swift puts it out, then I'm going to listen to it.

My hands are shaking when my driver drops me off in front of the small hotel on mainstreet in Estes Park. I don't know what I'm going to do here, or what happens next, but I'll figure it out. That's what I do, I figure things out.

It's late, since I didn't even land until almost nine. But after I get checked into my room, I walk down to the small grocery store on the corner that's still open.

Everything is fine until I hear a person yell. I can't tell if it's in jest or not, but I freeze and close my eyes, rocking back and forth on my feet, trying to remind myself to breathe.

"Are you alright?" I hear a woman's voice and my eyes fly open. A woman, just slightly taller than me, gives me a smile. She's older than me, though I can't tell by how much. But there's a sprinkling of gray hairs in her dark brown hair. "Are you alright?" she asks me again, and even though she's a stranger and I don't do well with strangers, I shake my head no.

The stranger takes my basket full of groceries and puts it in her cart. "We'll be back in a few, James," she hollers to one of the clerks and then she leads me outside. The shock of the cold air hits me but I'm still struggling to breathe.

The woman leads me to a bench and sits beside me.

"Follow my breath," she says and I try to focus as she counts to four, again and again, breathing in and out until my heart rate slows and I feel embarrassed.

"Thanks," I say and instead of looking judgemental, she smiles at me.

"You're welcome. I'm Hannah by the way. And I'm no

stranger to panic attacks in public places. It always helps me to get outside and focus on breathing, that at least keeps the panic at bay."

I look at Hannah curiously. "That was a panic attack?" It makes sense, and things start to connect in my mind—when Sam found me in the shower, the same thing had happened. I just don't know why it happened today.

Hannah nods. "Has it ever happened before?"

"A few days ago," I tell her, but it feels like it's been happening for much longer. I don't know why it seems so easy to open up to this stranger, but I don't feel like lying. I'm too exhausted.

"You just here for a vacation?" she asks me then.

I shake my head. "I don't think so. I'm not really sure what I'm doing next. But I couldn't stay in New York anymore, so I ended up here. I'm Annie."

"Nice to meet you," Hannah says. "My husband and I live about ten minutes from town, but I came to do our weekly grocery run tonight. We run a summer camp that helps kids who have anxiety and depression and do hikes in the summer as well. It's the off season now, so we've been sharing videos online about how we homestead, even in the winter. Anyway, that's a lot of information to give a person you just met."

I smile at her, she's giving off good vibes.

"Can I give you my number? If you need anything, I'd love to help. I can even give you the name and number of my therapist, unless that's too weird. You can tell me if that's too weird. I tend to be an oversharer, especially about mental health things."

"It's not weird, surprisingly," I tell her. I'm not sure a therapist is what I want or even need, but it is nice of her to offer. I didn't exactly grow up in a home where mental health was ever talked about. I don't know enough about any of it to know what I need.

She tells me her phone number and I send her a text so she'll have my number too. I was so worried about how hard it would be to meet new people here, but I guess my panic attack was kind of kismet.

We walk back into the store together, and I'm still feeling a bit jittery. I'll just check out what I have in my basket and head back to my hotel.

"Thanks," I tell Hannah before I walk away. "For helping a stranger."

"You're welcome," she smiles before pushing her cart away.

___

24

SAM

March 2024

I stare into the camera for the last time. My camera guy, Luke, sits on one of the stools in my kitchen and I take a deep breath. Time to film my last video for YouTube.

"Hey fellow travelers," I start my rehearsed speech. "This video is going to be a little different than the videos in my past. You might have noticed that I've been posting less and less. And while I've loved my career here on YouTube and traveling the world, it's time to close this chapter on my life.

"I know not everyone is going to be happy with that decision, but it's the right one for me. Last year, I had back surgery and while I can still travel, the injury was a wakeup call to me. It's time for me to settle down and have a family instead of traveling all the time. Thanks for being here. Thanks for traveling with me. Thanks for watching my videos throughout the years. The videos won't be going anywhere, I just won't be posting anymore."

I stop, unsure of how to end my comments.

"Happy travels." I offer a wave and Luke turns the camera off.

"It's been a pleasure working for you man," he tells me as he gets things packed up.

"Likewise." I gave all of my employees fantastic recommendations and they were all able to find new positions. Which makes me feel less guilty. They depended on me, but I'm quitting. It's weird, after years and years of sharing my life online, I'm going to be done. I know it is the right thing for me to do, but it's going to take some time to adjust to the new normal.

After Luke leaves, I check my phone. Every day, I seem to be waiting to hear from Annie, but she never texts and she never calls. I want to worry about how she's doing, but I also am trusting that she's doing what she needs to so that she and I can actually be together. But more than the worry, I miss her. I miss talking to her and hearing her laugh. I got so used to seeing her everyday, it's still a shock every day that I spend in this empty apartment.

I stare at my phone, willing for a text to come through, and to my surprise, one does. But it's not from Annie.

Maybe Chiara: Hi Sam, this is Chiara. I used to work with Annie and she gave me your phone number when I reached out to her last week. I've been putting together a list of documents, photos, and comments from other coworkers of ours to build a case against Mitch Austen. Would you be interested in meeting and talking about anything you remember that happened with Annie? I know that's a lot. She said she doesn't want to be involved with anything relating to him right now, which I get, but it would be helpful to get an eyewitness of the aftermath.

I stare at my phone dumbly. Didn't Annie tell Noah that she already reported Mitch? And that the cops wouldn't do anything?

Me: I'm happy to chat. Free anytime. Let me know when and where.

I may as well ask my questions to Chiara, maybe she'll have some answers.

☼

"Hi, thanks for meeting with me." Chiara stands as I walk toward her table. We met briefly—once—a few years ago after she started working at Austen's, but that time in my life is a little fuzzy.

I shake her hand. "Of course."

We both sit and she clasps her hands in front of her. "I put in my two weeks right after Annie left and told me what had happened. But because she was gone and I was the highest chef at Austen's, I've been staying on to train the new chef. She's young, twenty-three. And I noticed about a week after she started, that Mitch started to take a special interest in her."

My jaw clenches, but I keep listening.

"I don't believe anything has happened yet, but I did tell her about Annie—with her permission—and the new chef told me she'll let me know if anything happens. But I'd like to stop anything from ever happening, to anyone ever again."

I nod. "That's smart."

"I have a friend who works at one of the precincts here, so she's helping me out to build a case against Mitch. If you could share anything about where you were and when you saw things happening with Annie, that would be great. I'll record you if you don't mind."

"That's fine."

She puts her phone on the table between us, and I tell her everything that I remember.

"Thanks again for meeting with me," Chiara says as we stand to go.

"You're welcome." I shove my hands into the front pockets of my jeans. "I do have one question though. Why are you doing all this if Annie reported after he hit her? She told her brother she'd reported everything and that they weren't doing anything."

Chiara looks sad. "She didn't ever report. She wanted to keep her job, and so she didn't report because she didn't want to rock the boat. My guess is that she told her brother that so he'd get off her back."

That's what I thought. "Thanks."

I walk home slowly, feeling the weight of our conversation. Annie must have felt like she had to deal with everything all alone. "You're killing me, sunshine," I say to myself. I want to be there for her, but I can't be unless she lets me in. When I see her again, I'll show her that I'm all in. That no matter what, I'm going to be there for her. That she doesn't need to run away when things get hard.

Because I'm not going anywhere.

25

ANNIE

March 2024

The couch in my therapist's office is huge and threatens to swallow me whole so I perch on the edge like I'm about to jump up and run out of here. Really though, I'd like to sink into it, but I know if I do that, then I won't do any talking.

"How have things been going?" Dawn asks me. This is our fifth session together. I told her all about my mom and Mitch and my history with Sam in the past few sessions and she's given me a few coping skills to help when I get triggered and so far, they have been helping. Grounding myself in the present is the one thing that seems to help the most. Either looking around the room or wherever I am and noticing what's around me or turning on my favorite Taylor Swift song and dancing around. Getting out of my head and into the present moment is the one thing that keeps most of the flashbacks at bay.

Talking about what happened is exhausting, but it feels good to talk about it at the same time. Therapy is weird. Helpful, but weird.

"I'm okay." I twist my hands nervously. "I almost called Sam last night." We haven't talked much about Sam, but Dawn knows that he's my husband and that he loves me.

"Tell me about it," Dawn encourages gently.

"I was feeling a little lonely, now that I'm all moved into the cabin on Hannah's property. I don't see as many people as I did when I was at the hotel, but I like the solitude for the most part. Mostly I just wanted to call Sam and tell him all about my life, but I'm not ready to invite him into it, so I don't feel like I can call him."

Dawn nods slowly. "Are you afraid of what could happen if you do let him in?"

"I don't want to get hurt again," I tell her truthfully. "But I know that Sam won't hurt me the way that Mitch did."

"But he's still human, he'll still hurt you."

"I know. I just don't want to hurt him. I don't want to put all of this on him." I gesture to myself. I don't want to put the panic attacks and flashback nightmares where I wake up sweating and screaming on Sam. He doesn't need that kind of stress."

"Why would you put it on him?"

"I mean, he'd be my husband and he'd worry about me and I don't want him to worry."

"Shouldn't that be up to him to decide?" Dawn asks.

I shift uncomfortably. "I don't know."

"Why don't you think about it? I think that Sam could be another great support to you."

"I love him," I blurt out. "But I don't want to. I don't feel like he should love me either, I'm too much of a mess."

"Do you think that maybe because of how your mom treated you growing up, and her past relationships, made you feel as though you aren't worthy of love?" Dawn asks and I meet her eyes. How does she always know how to ask the questions that hit me straight in the heart? It's like she knows more about my own brain and what's happening inside it than I do.

"I don't know." I glance down at my hands. "My mom is complicated, and I know that, but she always made me feel like a burden and so did Mitch."

"Has Sam ever made you feel that way?"

"Well, no, but..."

"I think there are some things you need to think about, to work through. There have been too many people in your life who haven't shown you what it means to be loved. But that doesn't mean that you aren't worthy of it. Sam has been in your life for fourteen years, maybe it's time to think about what that means and talk to him about what he wants in the future."

"I'm scared," I tell her.

"I know. Loving another person is one of the scariest things we can do. We give our hearts to them and hope like hell that they won't hurt us. They will though, because we're all human, but that doesn't mean we should run away from a love like the one you and Sam have."

I blink away the tears that spring to my eyes. "I'll think about it."

"I'm going to follow up in a few weeks. Give you time to sit with this. But I do think you should reach out to Sam and tell him your fears, give him a chance to love you. And let yourself love him."

PART THREE
PRESENT DAY

26

ANNIE

I'm staring and I know it. But I haven't seen Sam in six months, not since I told him I was leaving to start something new and he didn't follow me—because I asked him not to. I watch as Sam, my husband—I suppress a shiver at the reminder—takes me in, all of me, from head to toe. He's looking at me as if he can't believe that I'm alive, that I'm here, that I'm real. To be honest, I kind of feel the same way about him. Everything is different now, for so many reasons. But it's good to see him.

I just don't know if he's forgiven me or if he will forgive me for the way I left things and I'm not really sure what to do about that.

"Want to come in?" I don't know how I manage to find the words, but I do. I open the door wider so he can make his way into the room. There's a small kitchen right as you walk in, and the door to the massive bathroom. Inside the room area is a king size bed and a couch that I'm hoping turns into a bed for Sam's sake. While I slept the best I've ever slept with Sam by my side, I don't know if he feels the same way, especially now.

"Nice place," Sam says, dropping his bag by the window,

and looking out over one of the resort's pools. "Did Noah tell you his flight was canceled?"

I nod, my brain is trying to catch up with my body. I have the irresistible urge to go and hug Sam, but that would make everything confusing. We're married and I left. He knows that, I know that. But my heart is pounding in my stomach and roaring in my ears and it's all I can do to not move to him and wrap my arms around him.

I feel safe these days. I'm doing much better thanks to therapy, getting out of New York, and moving to Estes Park. I can't help but wonder if I'd still feel safe in his embrace, if things could be different between us, if he even wants that anymore.

"I just got off the phone with Noah. He asked if I was okay with you staying here with me, since you can't get into your room with it under his name." I know I'm regurgitating information and that he already knows this since he showed up at my door.

"Is it okay that I'm here?" he asks me quietly, so quietly like he's afraid to be in my space. I take a step closer to him.

"It's okay." I meet his eyes. "But you will be sleeping on the couch bed."

"Of course." His grin makes me want to hug him or be hugged by him, but I hold myself back as he says, "I want you to be comfortable."

My heart feels like it breaks into a million pieces at his words. He's not supposed to worry about me still.

"I'm good," I tell him and I mean it. "I'm sorry I haven't called."

"Where did you end up?" Sam asks me, looking out the window again and ignoring my apology.

"Estes Park," I tell him. "I just signed a lease for a restaurant space."

Sam whirls around, grinning. He takes two steps toward me

before slowing his pace, hesitant to reach out and touch me. "That's incredible, sunshine."

My stomach swirls at the nickname. When did Noah say he'd be getting here? I don't know if I'll make it with Sam as my only companion here for the next thirty or so hours.

"Did you pick a name for it yet?" Sam asks me.

"No, that's still a work in progress." Actually, a lot of it is a work in progress. I need to find a business manager to help with all of the logistics. I can make great food, but I am not a savvy business person. "I'm looking for a manager right now to help with everything. I know how to do the food part, but not anything else."

This is part of the reason why starting my own restaurant took so long, because I don't really like letting people into my circle, and finding someone to go into business with seems like a huge task. Plus, I haven't really been ready until this point.

Sam looks at me curiously. "I've got a business degree. I can ask around to see if any of my buddies would be able to help."

Part of me wishes he'd offer himself, but that would be asking way too much. I couldn't do that to him. I wouldn't ask him to move away from his life in New York. To give up his life as a famous YouTuber. I haven't let myself check out his channel since I left. I broke my own heart and had to live with the pain.

Suddenly, these four walls around us feel too small for me and all the emotions I'm feeling. I should probably text my therapist and tell her that Sam is here and it'll just be the two of us until everyone else arrives tomorrow. She'll know what I should do. Actually, I can hear her voice in my head telling me that I should tell him how I feel, how I want to try again with him. But that feels like jumping off a cliff. So I don't reach for my phone.

"That would be great, thanks," I say. "Do you want to go get some food?"

"Sure," Sam answers, "Let me just freshen up a bit then we can head out."

He walks past me, careful not to touch me as he passes. I let out my breath as the door shuts behind him. I pull out my phone and text Emily and my friend Hannah from Estes Park.

Me: Sam is HERE. My brother's flight got CANCELED. I have to verify all the venue stuff with SAM. LOW KEY FREAKING OUT.

I don't expect to hear back from Hannah for a while. She runs a summer camp for kids with anxiety disorders and it takes pretty much all of her time these days. I try to think about what time it is in Colorado right now. Eight maybe? That means it's nearly time for the kids' bonfire at night. I went to the camp last week to help out before I came here. It was fun, and it's amazing what Hannah does for the kids.

And Emily is probably wrangling her kids into bed, so it'll be a bit before either one can respond. I flip my phone over.

Sam comes out of the bathroom. "Shall we?" he asks and I nod, getting up off the bed and following him out the door.

"There are some food trucks about half a mile walk from here," I tell him as we step out into the somewhat humid air. The salty smell of the ocean hits me like a wave and I feel like I can relax. I never thought I was an ocean person, but it turns out, I kind of really love it.

If it wasn't so dang expensive, I would come here for every vacation.

"Sound great," he says as he matches his pace with mine.

"How was your flight?" I ask. I also want to ask him what he's been up to these days, where he's traveled, and how his vlog is doing. I haven't let myself look him up at all since I left. I don't feel like that's my privilege to know anymore. I left him.

The shame of it all washes over me—again—and I try to push it down. I knew he'd be here in Hawaii and I already planned to apologize. My therapist told me it's a good first step. She also told me—several times—that I need to tell him how I feel. I'll get there. I hope.

"Fine," he says. "Both were long, the layover in Los Angeles was fine, but that airport has way too many people."

"Which is exactly why I had a direct flight," I say, laughing a little. "I do not like dealing with layovers." I don't say I have to deal with one on the way home, I'll deal with that when I have to.

"How was your flight?" He asks. He knows I hate flying pretty much more than anything. Noah offered to buy me a ticket if I wanted to drive to Utah and fly out with him, but honestly, traveling with other people stresses me out way more. I'm then anxious for myself and for what they're going through. Are they mad that we're slightly delayed? Are they uncomfortable but just keeping it to themselves until something bigger happens and they blow up on me? I should probably talk to my therapist about these fears—the anxiety I feel for other people. It's probably related to Mitch and not knowing how he'd ever react to anything. But for those reasons, I like traveling alone, even if I hate traveling.

"Fine. I took a sleeping pill and slept the entire time."

"Good." Sam shoves his hands into the front pockets of his shorts, like he doesn't know what else to do with them. It's a habit he's always had and I want to reach over, pull his hand out and hold it. But I am too focused on breathing right now and not making everything awkward.

We fall into a semi-comfortable silence as we walk to the food trucks. I only know they exist because of Hannah. She's stayed at this resort before and told me all the best places to go eat and what to do while I'm here.

"Tomorrow we'll have to make sure everything is ready for the wedding," I say. "Noah asked if we could do that and I said yes. But that should only take an hour or so, then we can hang out by the pool or hike or whatever."

"Did you just offer to go hiking, sunshine?" He grins at me.

I flush. "I mean, I know you probably don't want to hang out at the pool all day." There I am, being what Taylor Swift called a pathological people pleaser. That's me.

"Actually, sitting by the pool sounds kind of nice. I brought a new mystery novel to read. It'll be nice to relax a bit before all the wedding craziness starts," Sam says.

"Only if you're sure." My heart squeezes. I don't want him to miss out on a chance at exploring the island simply because I'd rather sit by the pool and read.

Sam gives me a look that I can't quite read. It's like he knows what I'm trying to do, but isn't sure he wants to call me out on it. "I'm sure, sunshine."

27

———

SAM

I silently curse myself for using my nickname for her right now as I watch Annie's cheeks turn pink. I'm supposed to be mad at her, at least, I was for a few days after she left. But then I just missed her.

I've spent the past six months getting my life in order in case she called. I officially quit vlogging and while people are still less than thrilled that I quit YouTubing, I know it was the right call. It wasn't ever going to be the same, not after I had back surgery. I found everyone on my team a new position, it was the least that I could do. I just sold my apartment in New York and last week I drove to Colorado. I've been staying with my parents, not knowing that Annie was in the same state.

But I can't stay mad at her, I can't even pretend to be mad at her. I think she expects me to be mad, but I'm not. She looks stunning, light, and free. A version of herself that she hasn't been for a long time.

"There's pretty much anything you could possibly want to eat," she says as we walk to the field full of food trucks. In the end, we try a Thai place that ends up being fantastic.

"I could eat this every day," she says in delight as she eats her mango chicken salad.

I bite my cheek to keep from laughing. "I forgot how much watching you eat good food makes me happy."

She freezes. "Why does it make you happy?"

"You just unapologetically love the things that you love, and I love that about you." Yup, there goes my plan to pretend like we were just friends. I should have known it wouldn't have been possible. I can't be friends with her, especially not now that she's my wife.

She glances away as her cheeks and chest turn pink.

"Anyway," I say, I know that I need to change the subject. "What should we do after this?" The sun is slowly getting closer to the horizon.

"We could sit on the beach and watch the sunset," she suggests. "I did that last night and then promptly went to bed because I was so tired. But it was nice."

"That sounds like a perfect idea." And romantic, but I'm going to take this slow, show her that I'm going to be here for her in whatever way she needs.

"Unless there is something else you want to do," Annie rushes to say and I want to reach out and tell her to stop worrying so much about making sure I'm happy. Of course I'm happy, after six months, I am finally with her in person. And there isn't anything better than that.

"I'd just like to enjoy being with you," I finally say.

ANNIE

What the? My heart seems to decide that this is proof that maybe he has forgiven me, and that maybe he and I could really be together. Something that I haven't dared hope for in the past six months. Mainly because relationships have always been hard for me, but even harder after Mitch. I don't want to drag anyone down with my own screwed up mental health. I'm a lot, and I know that and I don't want to bring Sam down.

"Okay," I say, because I'm not sure what else to say. I should tell him now, all the things in my head that I've been thinking about for months but haven't had the courage to say aloud yet. But I don't.

"Okay," he echoes my reply back to me. And just like that, it's decided, the two of us are going to officially spend time together. Something we haven't done since I was in New York, since those perfect two days with Sam. I feel myself go warm all over with the memory.

I don't know what to say now. I feel like something slipped inside of me and turned off my ability to speak, even though I was supposed to be finding my voice again.

"This is hard for me," I tell him as we stand to throw away our garbage.

He freezes. "Me being here?"

I shake my head. "No. Yes. I'm just not sure what to say."

He nods like this makes sense. Then he smiles at me and I know he's about to tease me. "You could always say, 'I'm sorry I freaked out and ran away when things got to real and felt like I had to deal with all my hard things on my own.' That might be a good place to start."

I swallow. I am sorry I ran away, but can I actually say those words? "I am sorry, Sam."

He closes his eyes when I say his name, as if me saying his name does something to him. When he opens his eyes and looks at me, his eyes are clear and bright.

"Apology accepted," he says as we start to make our way back toward the beach.

I'm stuck for a moment, then I run to catch up with him. "Wait, really?"

"What did you expect, Annie?" he asks me, looking at me curiously. It's so strange to hear my name from his lips, he never uses my first name. I want him to call me sunshine. "Did you really expect me to hold a grudge? I know that you went through a whole lot of crap in New York that you never told me about. That day I found you in the shower? That was one of the scariest days of my life. The days after were practically perfect, but I still don't blame you for running, not at all. I just wish you'd told me you were going."

I swallow thickly. "Why?"

He stops walking and his green eyes seem to shoot straight through my heart. "So I could have been your getaway driver. So you could have known you don't have to keep facing all this stuff," he gestures at nothing, "alone. You aren't alone anymore."

My heart is pounding in my head. "I'm not?" I ask in a small voice.

He shakes his head, a stray hair comes loose from his bun. "Of course not, sunshine, now you've got a husband." He stuffs his hands in his pockets, as if what he just said didn't mean anything at all, as if it's just this light hearted truth, that I have a husband. That I'm his wife.

I'm too stunned to speak. I don't know whether he's being serious or not right now. I should take the leap, but it still feels too scary. I know he's always been around, as my friend, but this feels different. "You know it's just on paper, right?"

He doesn't look at me when he speaks next, and it's probably a good thing I can't see his face. "It's never been just on paper for me, Annie."

There it is with my name again. My stomach flips.

"What do you mean?" I know exactly what he means, but I need him to say the words. I want him to say the words, even if they terrify me.

"I don't think we're ready for that conversation," Sam answers, his voice quieter now, more reverent.

"When, then?" I ask. In five days, I go back to Colorado and he goes back to New York. But he's right, I'm not ready for this conversation. I may never be ready for this conversation. It's terrifying to let yourself fall for someone, especially after the relationship I had before this. I need to move slowly, but I also need to be honest.

He shrugs, looking ahead of us on the path. We're surrounded by people, but I have"t really noticed any of them. It's like it's just me and him.

"Soon, I hope," is all he says, then he changes the subject. "Should we find a spot to watch the sunset?"

I nod, and follow him onto the beach. Hopefully, I can talk about everything I feel for him while we're here. Hopefully, I can be brave.

28

ANNIE

"Well, this is a problem." We both stare at the couch that's supposed to turn into a bed. But no matter what we do, the bed won't come out. It's like the couch ate it and the hotel gods want us to sleep in the same bed.

"It's stuck," I say, for the seventh time. "I don't think we're getting it out."

"I'm going to try one more time." He's determined to make this work, but it's not working. That couch is not turning into a bed and I can tell he's exhausted. We watched the sunset and then got some ice cream on our way back to our room. But it's past midnight at home, and Sam likes to go to bed early, I'm just waiting for him to snap. He has to be so tired.

"One more time," he mutters to himself again as he grabs hold of the rope and handle to pull the hide-a-bed out of the couch. Then he stands there.

"I thought you said one more time," I say, watching him.

He grunts. "I'm trying."

I bite my lip to hold in my laughter. "The bed is a king, Sam. It'll be fine."

At least, that's what I'm telling myself. It will be fine, totally fine. I'm sure not thinking about all those things he said earlier, about how our marriage isn't just on paper for him or about how he kissed me the last time we were together. Nope, absolutely not going there.

"I'll just sleep on the couch," he argues as he puts the cushions back on. "It'll be fine."

"You need a bed." There is no way his back will be fine if he has to curl up on the hard, small couch all night. "You can just sleep on top of the covers with the extra blankets for the couch bed, and I'll sleep under them. It's a memory foam mattress, we won't even bug each other."

He sighs, resigned. "I don't want to make you uncomfortable."

I smile at him. "I'm good. Let's sleep. We have a busy morning." I move to the right side of the bed, the furthest from the door and unfold the covers. I climb into bed and pat the side beside me. "Come on, I won't bite."

He hesitates for a second before he moves to the other side of the bed. He fluffs the pillow and unfolds the extra comforter that was in the closet. The bed shifts slightly at the weight of him and I take a slow, deep breath. It's just Sam, this is going to be fine.

There is a mountain of blankets between us when I wake up around three in the morning, and I'm drenched with sweat. I wrack my mind for any nightmares, but for the first time in a long time, I was actually having a good dream. One about Sam. I groan and force myself to get up and out of bed to look at the air conditioner, because I cannot sleep when it's hot. I blink against the darkness, only to see Sam's silhouette by the window, at the AC unit already.

"What's happening?" I ask him as I yawn. He doesn't look at me, he pushes another button on the AC unit and nothing happens.

"It sputtered to a stop about an hour ago and now it won't turn back on. I'll call the front desk to see if we can get moved to a different room." He moves soundlessly around me and turns on a lamp on the table and presses the numbers needed to get to the front desk.

"Hi, yes. I'm in room 1203 and our air conditioner just stopped working. I see. Can we get moved to another room?" I watch Sam as he talks to whoever is on the other side of the phone, grateful it's him and not me, because I do not like talking to people on the phone.

And you're sure you can't move us to a different room?"

My heart sinks. There is no way I'm going to be able to sleep now. It's way too hot in here. I'm surprised I didn't wake up earlier. But I'm exhausted from yesterday.

"Okay, thank you," Sam says then he hangs up the phone and looks at me. "So they are aware there is a problem, I guess their entire AC system is currently down. They are bringing someone in soon to get it fixed, but it might be a bit."

I swallow the panic rising in my chest. I am still not great at adapting when things don't go the way I anticipate.

"So, we'll open the sliding door. We're high enough up that it shouldn't be a problem, and I'm going to see if there's a fan in the closet, the guy at the desk said there should be. And if all else fails, we can fill up the tub with cold water and dunk ourselves to feel cooler."

I relax a tad. "Okay."

He smiles at me. "It's going to be alright, sunshine."

I nod, even though I don't believe him. I'm closest to the sliding door, so I open it and let in the humid, but slightly cooler night air. When I turn around, Sam is holding a small box fan that is probably older than the both of us, but it'll be better than nothing. At least we still have electricity. At least we had AC to start with. He plugs the fan in and sets it on the dresser across from the bed and turns it on.

It's pitiful, the amount of air it moves, but at least there's some sort of air flow.

He turns off the lamp, plunging the room in darkness again. We shuffle past each other to get to our sides of the bed. He pushes all of the blankets off the bed and I feel the tiny movement of air as I lay back down on my pillow.

"Is it okay if I scoot a tiny bit closer to you?" Sam asks. "I won't touch you, and we don't exactly need to share body heat, but I'd like to kind of feel the fan."

"Sure," I hear myself saying. I'm still sweating a lot. He shifts so he's closer to me, then he sits up and surprises me. He pulls off his shirt.

"Wh-what are you doing?" It's not like I've never seen the man shirtless, I have, many times. I can't even see him right now, not really because of the dark, and he even slept in the bed next to me without a shirt six months ago. But everything feels different now.

I can hear his smile. "It's hot. I'll keep my shorts on though."

"Thanks," I murmur, my body getting warmer than it was a second ago. Now, not only am I sharing a bed with my husband, he's also completely shirtless. For a half second, I wonder what would happen if I reach out and touch him. He's close enough that I easily could. But I don't. I clench my fists and keep my hands at my sides.

"Well, sleep well," he says into the darkness.

"Mhm," I murmur back, because fat chance of that happening.

The sun is bright when I open my eyes because at some point, despite being hot and hyper-aware of Sam in the bed beside me, I fell back asleep.

And then had a super detailed romantic dream about him. I blush just thinking about it.

Thankfully, he's in the shower, so I have a second to get my bearings before I see him. "It was just a dream," I tell myself, but I can't help but wonder what it would be like to have him kiss me like he was in my dream...to have him do more than kiss me.

"Nope. Nope Nope," I say as I pull out my phone. Better to distract myself than let myself think dirty thoughts about my husband.

I have three new texts. The first is from Noah, confirming that he and everyone else will be getting in late tonight and that he'll see us in the morning tomorrow. The others are from Hannah and Emily.

Emily: KISS HIM! Or I DON'T KNOW, tell him how you feel! And keep me posted.

Hannah: DID YOU KISS HIM YET?!?! And send me a picture, cause like... I don't know what he looks like.

I laugh. I haven't told Hannah that she could easily look up Sam online and know exactly what he looks like, but I'm not ready for that yet. I send her a text back.

Me: No kissing will be happening (except in my dreams apparently). We slept in the same bed last night, but nothing happened so keep your mind out of the gutter. I will not be telling him anything. I am here for my brother's wedding, not here to figure out my crap with Sam.

While I'm typing out the same message to Emily, Hannah responds.

Hannah: GO KISS THE MAN! And I want a SELFIE of the two of you. PLEASE. I'll put it on my fridge. Graham will die of joy to know that you're happy with your husband. You should tell him how you feel, even if you're there for your brother!

Me: No selfies for you.

The shower turns off, which means in the next ten minutes I'll see Sam. The same man who was just in my dreams. The one I have to spend the entire day with. No. Hannah would tell me to reframe that, the one I get to spend the entire day with. Maybe I should just relax and enjoy the day. I can pretend that everything is the same as it was before I ran away.

Sam comes out of the bathroom, a bunch of steam following him, in nothing but a towel.

"Oh."

His head whips to mine, and I really should look away, but I can't stop staring. He's got abs for days. And that V that people talk about on men, yup, he's got that too. I've seen him shirtless and in shorts before. But that was nothing compared to this. Him in a towel? I think I'm gawking. But I've never let myself really look at him before and now I can't seem to take my eyes off of him. I force myself to look at his face, but that's even worse, because he's watching me with an amused expression.

He caught me ogling him. The last time he and I were in this situation I didn't open my eyes until he went into his room, but now I just stare at this man like he is a delicious treat I can't wait to have. What is wrong with me?

"I didn't realize you were awake," he says.

"I didn't realize you were a Greek god," I reply, my face flaming. Cursed fair skin and my inability to hide a blush. "I, uh, you must have been working out a lot?"

There is no saving me from this. This is the second time in

my life that we've found ourselves in this position and I'm making it much, much worse than the first time.

He is still watching me, a smile on his face.

"Can you please put some clothes on?" I ask him before I bury my face in my hands. "Please."

He doesn't reply, but I hear him rummage through his suitcase. I don't dare look up again until the bathroom door clicks shut.

I bite back a smile as we head down to the front desk where we're supposed to talk to a woman named Kelly about wedding details. From what Noah told me, the resort is handling pretty much everything, so today should just be a tour of where the ceremony will be and going over the menu for the reception one last time.

The look that Annie gave me this morning was priceless. I really didn't know she was awake and I hadn't wanted to wake her up by rummaging through my suitcase before I showered so I figured I could just sneak back out when I was done and maybe, with more light from the sun, grab my clothes before she woke up. But then I caught her looking at me—staring at me like she wanted to reach out and touch me. And well, let's just say I'm a happy man.

Even if she won't look at me right now—which makes it all better, because that means she's still attracted to me.

"So, how are you doing, in general I mean?" I ask at the same time Annie says, "You ready for the wedding activities?"

She shuffles her feet and looks down at the floor while we wait for the elevator. "I'm doing okay, going to therapy now."

"That's good," I say. I want to ask about how she's doing—without me—if she's got an ache in her heart like I do while we've been a part, but I also don't want to scare her off. "And yeah, I'm ready for the wedding. Noah's finally getting married."

Annie grins up at me. A sight that makes my heart leap in relief. We can do this. We're still us. "He's finally getting married. He said that today they'll show us where the ceremony will take place, as well as the reception thing after. I'm not really sure what to call it. It's a reception or a late lunch or an early dinner."

"One of those things," I say as we walk into the elevator. I hit the lobby button. I imagine it'll end up happening later than it's planned, only because that seems to be how things always go. Everything takes longer than you expect.

"Yup. So we have to go through everything, make sure it all looks good. I don't think we have to check on the food, since it's just at a restaurant. But we should have the afternoon free."

Free to hang out, I hope.

We fall into a more comfortable silence as we walk to the lobby. I want to ask Annie more about therapy, but there will be time later to talk about it. To see how she's really doing. I can't tell if she's got her guard up because I'm me and everything that's happened between us, or because of everything that happened with Mitch. I honestly hope it's because of me, because maybe I can fix that.

But even if it's because of Mitch, I'll be here for Annie, in whatever way she lets me be.

I give the woman behind the counter a friendly smile as we approach and she assesses me and Annie. I can already tell the type of person she is. She's going to try to flirt with me.

"Hi, we're here to discuss all the arrangements for the Nelson/Jones wedding tomorrow," I say.

Just like I guessed, she flutters her eyes up at me with a wry grin. "Welcome." She doesn't bother looking at Annie. "I'm Erica and I'll be able to assist you. I think Kelly was originally going to help you, but she's out sick today."

"Well thanks," I say and then I touch the small of Annie's back, and she glances up at me in surprise.

The woman's face cools, slightly. "Right this way, Mr. Jones and Ms. Nelson."

Annie opens her mouth to correct her, but I squeeze her side. "Just go with it," I whisper. It'll be easier than trying to explain to this stranger what's happening. Plus, maybe she'll stop with the obvious flirting.

I move my hand and take Annie's hand in mine. She doesn't pull away. I meant what I said last night about her not being ready for the full conversation about how I feel about her and how she feels about me. But we're going to have it and we're going to have it soon. Until then, I want to show her how I feel. The one thing I do know how to do is show her how much I love her.

Without being obnoxious or crossing any lines, I told her back in New York that we could take it slow, and I'll take it slow now. I want us to fall in love with each other.

Erica leads us down a long hallway and then out the door leading to a small courtyard. "The ceremony will be on one of our more secluded lawns. It will be blocked off for the duration of the ceremony, so it should be quite nice."

It's stunning, much more romantic than the courthouse where Annie and I were married. If I get a chance to do that part over, I'd love to do it in a place like this or in the mountains.

"There is no pool on this side, so it should be quiet. You have your marriage certificate, I assume?" Erica asks.

"Yup," I say. "We got it when we got here, so we're all ready for Friday, just have to wait for the rest of our guests to get here."

"Lovely," Erica says, and I can tell by her tone that she doesn't think it's lovely, not one bit. She seems less than thrilled that I'm off the market, but is she for real? It would take a lot more than a five minute conversation for me to be interested in any one person except maybe Annie. I might have fallen in love with her the moment I saw her. It was like my soul knew that I was meant to be hers and she was meant to be mine right from the start. It took time to get here, but it was worth every minute.

"And the beach front restaurant for the dinner, where is that?" I ask, looking at Annie. She's been quiet all morning and seems to be growing more tense with each moment we spend with Erica. The sooner we can finish this, the better.

"Right this way." Erica leads us to the boardwalk where we walk a little ways down to a restaurant. She points, "There is a private deck here that you booked which will be yours for the evening."

"Thank you," I tell her. "Is there anything else we need to do or know?"

"We'll take care of the rest," Erica tells us. "But if you have any questions, any at all, give me a call and I'll be able to get everything sorted."

Erica hands me a business card, and her fingers purposely brushing mine. Annie stills beside me. As Erica leaves, I turn to Annie.

"You alright?: I ask, giving her my full attention. I know she's not, but I want her to tell me.

She gives me the slightest head shake.

"What do you need?: I ask her and watch as she looks out at the water.

"Can you just hug me for a second?" she asks, voice quiet.

"Of course." I pull her into my arms and look over her head

out at the ocean. Her heart is racing as I tighten my hold. After a few minutes, her heart rate slows.

"Want to tell me what happened?" I ask.

"I'm not exactly sure," she answers. "Something about that lady reminded me of..." Annie takes a slow, deep breath. "My body just kind of freaked out. My therapist warned me that this would still happen, that things would trigger me even if I didn't understand it. That my nervous system would go into fight or flight mode, even when I'm not actually in danger."

"And me hugging you helps?" I ask as she touches the front of my shirt.

"Anything that grounds me in the present and reminds me that I am safe helps, but yeah, physical touch like a hug or someone squeezing my hand, those things help the fastest."

"Well, I'm happy I was here to help, sunshine." I lean forward and press a kiss to her temple. She closes her eyes.

"Thank you for making me feel safe, Sam," Annie whispers. "You've always been good at that."

"You're welcome," I whisper back and something like hope swells inside my chest. There might be hope for the two of us after all.

I feel Annie take a deep breath against me, as if she's preparing herself to say something big. "I'm going to have to move slowly."

"Slow is great." I reassure her.

She looks up at me, her eyes glinting in the morning sun. I know I just told her that slow is great, but I'd really like to kiss her right now.

"I don't want to freak you out," I tell her, "But I do want to see what happens with us. But I'm willing to go at your pace. You can hold all the reigns."

She nods. "It's not going to be easy for you. I'm a hot mess." She lets out a small laugh. "But I'm trying. Therapy has been helping a lot. I'm learning more about myself and why I fell into the trap that was Mitch and why it was so hard to leave, even when he was horrible. I'm not ready to talk about all those things with you though."

I squeeze her hips with my hands. "That's okay."

"Is it?"

"Of course. I would love if you could come and talk to me about all the hard stuff, but if you're not ready for that—or even if you never get there—that's okay. I'm going to still be here. And I'll drive you to therapy so that you can talk to someone."

She swallows and looks away from me. Out toward the ocean.

"You're holding the reigns, okay?" I give her another hug.

"Okay. Thanks, Sam" When she smiles up at me, it's just like all those years ago when we first starting hanging out. A ray of sunshine straight to my chest. I smile back at her.

30

ANNIE

"Ready to hit the pool?" I ask Sam as I leave his warm embrace and he watches me carefully. He's giving me the power and control in our relationship and honestly, I don't know what to do with it. I'm proud of myself for telling him about therapy and sharing that I'm not quite ready to share everything with him.

But I do want to move forward with him, even if it's slow. I'm glad he's letting me take it slow.

"I am if you are," he says.

I nod. "Let's do it. I could use a relaxing day." Understatement of the year, honestly, but when in Maui you should relax, right? Plus, I feel like a huge weight was lifted now that I know he's not going to pressure me into anything. Not that I ever thought he would, but it's nice to know we can move at my pace.

"Then a relaxing day is what you'll get." We make our way back to the hotel room, where he lets me get ready first. I pull on my two piece swimsuit, the first one I've felt comfortable in in years. That's another thing I'm learning, that it might take years for me to feel comfortable in my own body again. Mitch's words did so much harm that it's hard for me to be in my own skin. I generally like to hide under baggy clothes or my chef's uniform.

Hiding under my clothes means that people don't look at me. Wearing a two piece swimsuit—even one that has pretty decent coverage—is still way out of my comfort zone. I want to take back my body and I know this is one way I can do that.

Hannah and Emily would be proud. Chiara would probably be proud too, but I don't talk to her as much right now. She told me she's building a case against Mitch, which I think is great, but I also can't handle it right now so she and I haven't talked much since I left New York beyond her telling me about what she's doing.

I pull on shorts and a T-shirt before heading out into the main room where Sam sits at the table, waiting. "It's all yours," I say.

I almost tell him that I'll head down by myself to find some lounge chairs for us, but in the end I sit on my bed and scroll through Instagram while I wait for him to be ready.

We end up a little ways away from the pool, but we can see the ocean from our chairs, so I'm happy. "I'm going to go walk by the beach for a minute."

He hesitates a moment. "Do you want me to come with you?"

I shake my head. "I'll be back in like ten minutes."

"If you aren't, I'll send out a search party."

I bite back a smile. "You would do that."

"Gotta know where my wife is if she doesn't come back when she says she will." His words hit me straight in my heart. I want to tell him I'm sorry for staying in Colorado, for not going back to New York like I said I would once I found myself more. But I can't bring myself to say those words. Because I don't think I'll ever go back to New York and even though he gave me the reigns, I'm not sure I can push past the guilt I feel about asking him to come back to Colorado with me. New York is his home now.

"I'll be back," I promise him, and this time I mean it.

Once I hit the sand, I slip off my sandals and hold them as I walk toward the water. There's a family playing frisbee and a couple of men throwing a football. But it's still pretty early, so there aren't many people out on the beach yet.

The water is cool as it rushes against my ankles, covering my feet. But it feels good. I close my eyes and relish the feeling. There's something about the ocean that makes me feel so incredibly alive. I open my eyes and watch the waves for a few minutes, letting my mind clear.

I wish I could do this every day. Visiting is nice, it's healing, but I probably couldn't live by the ocean all the time. It's big and vast and while incredible, it also freaks me out if I think about it too much. I stand there for the rest of my ten minute walk, just relishing in the feel of the water against my ankles, the fastness of the ocean, and how calm it all makes me feel in this moment.

I'm still a little jittery from my weird panic moment I had earlier. I don't know if I'll ever get used to this—feeling anxiety—but maybe I'm not supposed to get used to it. Dawn told me that it was going to take time before seemingly random things didn't trigger me as often, if at all. But it's part of the healing process.

I take a deep breath. I'm okay. I'm more than okay. Sam is here and I have a therapist and good friends and a new life. I'm okay.

I make my way back up to the resort, even though I want to stay by the water. I don't want Sam to worry about me.

"Ah, back with one minute to spare." Sam grins at me. He's got his shirt off now and I flush, remembering this morning. "How was the water?"

"It was perfect." I sit down in the chair and ask, "Promise me something?"

"Anything, sunshine," he says.

"That you'll bring me back here every year, even if things don't work out between us." I don't want to sound like a pessimist, I'm just trying to be realistic. Sam is going to wake up and realize one day that I can't give him the life he wants and he'll leave.

"Every year," he promises. "Even when we're old and gray."

I smile at him. "Thank you."

"No, thank you," Sam says.

"For what?"

"For everything."

Before I get a chance to ask what he means, a waiter comes by and gives us the poolside brunch menu. "I'll be back in a moment to see if you want anything."

"I'm not hungry yet," I tell Sam. "But you can get something if you want. I'm going to go jump in the pool for a second before I sit out here in the sun so I don't get too hot."

"Want me to help with your sunscreen?" he asks as I pull off my shirt. He doesn't even try to hide the fact that he's checking me out, and for some reason, I don't mind. Lately, I've avoided any man looking in my direction, but I watch as he takes me in. When his eyes meet mine again, there's a reverent sort of look in them, like he can't believe that I let him look at me that way.

"Sure," I say, hoping my voice sounds normal. I slip off my shorts and turn around for him to get my shoulders and my back. His fingers are soft and his touch is gentle as he starts to rub on the sunscreen. I nearly lean into his touch, it feels so good. I have to bite the inside of my cheek to not do anything drastic—like turn around and kiss him like my life depended on it. Because that's really what I want to do with his hands all over my back.

Once he's done, I do my face and arms. When I drop the bottle on my seat, I can feel his eyes on me again.

"Can I help you?: I ask in a joking voice.

"Your tattoo." He points to my exposed hip bone. I didn't realize how low these bottoms sit on my body until now. But my tiny tattoo is peeking out over the waistband.

"What about it?" I ask. I know why he's asking, it's the sun. The *same sun* from the ring he gave me all those years ago. And he calls me sunshine, he's the only one that calls me sunshine.

He looks at me, his eyes wild. I've never seen him like this.

"It's just a tattoo, Sam," I say, trying to brush it off. Maybe I should tell him about it, but maybe I want him to wonder about it a little more.

"Right," he says, his voice gruff. "It's just a tattoo."

I nod, satisfied that I've got him so discombobulated. Join the club my friend. "I'll be back in a few," I say and then I head toward the pool. After I jump in and look over to our spot, I can tell that he is still in the same position that I left him in.

This makes me smile.

When I get back to our chairs, his eyes are closed. He still has his shirt off and I allow myself ten seconds to look at him. He's as beautiful as he's always been.

By the time he opens his eyes again, I'm back in my shirt and shorts. How could I have forgotten that he didn't know about the tattoo? I'm still not ready to talk about it. Not with Sam.

Not yet.

"You hungry?" Sam sits up and stretches and I have to avert my gaze as I feel myself grow warm remembering this morning. I want to close my eyes and forget those gorgeous abs. And my silly Greek god comment.

"I could eat," I say.

"A lady was just talking about some good pancakes at a

place across the street from the food trucks. We could go if you're up for a walk."

"Sure."

Really though, I just keep waiting for the urge to run to hit me. I know it's going to come because that's what always happens to me. When things get too real or too deep, I run. I did it with Sam when we were younger. I did it when I ran away from my life in Colorado to start culinary school, even though Mom didn't want me to. I tried when I was with Mitch, but he didn't let me. And then I let him control so many parts of me for so long, that I'm only now starting to find myself again. I kept telling myself, when I got back to Colorado six months ago, that I was going to be different, that it was the last time I ran. That I could finally face my feelings and the harder things in life.

The real things.

But now that Sam is sitting beside, real as ever in that Greek god body of his and saying all sorts of things that confuse my brain and staring at my tattoo like he remembers that cheap ring he got me years ago...I feel like I should want to run.

And I do, but straight into his arms. I want this to be real between us. A real relationship for the first time ever, and a real marriage instead of one of convenience. And I don't have any idea what that means.

The pancake place is to die for. Sam orders a pineapple pancake ensemble and I order their original pancakes with hash-browns and eggs on the side. "We'll have to bring Noah and Tally here tomorrow morning," I say after I take my first bite.

"It is really good," he says. "Can I try yours? Mine are way too sweet."

We end up trading pancakes, because I love his and he prefers the normal ones.

"So, more pool time after this?"

"For sure." Sam grins and it's a glorious sight, I ignore the voice in my head that tells me I shouldn't get attached, that I shouldn't let his smile affect me so much. But part of me—the part that is so tired from running—wants to do more to stay close to him, to see what could happen between us if I let my real feelings show, for the first time ever, between us.

31

ANNIE

"Want to hang out in the hot tub tonight?" Sam asks as we walk back from dinner later that day.

"I guess," I say, but I don't particularly like hot tubs. They feel nice for about five minutes before I get too hot and too antsy and just want to get out. I personally don't understand the appeal.

"You don't have to do that, you know," he says bumping my shoulder with his.

"Do what?" I ask, looking up at him and I find him already looking down at me. Butterflies swirl in my stomach. Maybe someday I'll be able to tell him just exactly what his look does to me.

"Say yes even when you don't want to do something," Sam says.

I struggle to find words. "I want to. Kind of. But I don't really enjoy hot tubs much. For like less than ten minutes and then I just want to get in the pool."

Sam gives me an easy grin. "That's fine with me."

"Are you just saying that?" Growing up, I was always a people pleaser, then everything that happened with Mitch didn't really help that. Now I don't know how to balance saying yes to other people and doing more of what I want to do. And I worry that other people say yes to accommodate me, even when they don't want to and I hate that.

"Annie," Sam says and my stomach flips just like it always does whenever he says my name. "We already talked about this."

"I know, but—" Sam puts a finger to my lips. I stare up at his bright blue eyes.

"No buts. Just relax. We'll get warm in the hot tub and then swim in the pool. I honestly just want to hang out with you. Like we used to."

"I'm sorry," I murmur against his finger. It's my fault we stopped hanging out, I left.

Sam shakes his head. "None of that either. I know why you left. I just wish you'd have told me where you were going so I could have come."

I wish he had come with me. For the past month or so, I've been letting myself daydream about what a life with Sam would look like in Colorado. It'd be a fresh start for both of us.

I decide to be brave. "You could come now, if you wanted," I tell him and then I'm scrambling. I didn't mean to say that right this second, but I guess there's no time like the present. "I need a restaurant manager and you could still do your YouTube thing. I could give you great hours and you might like—"

Sam cuts me off again, this time with both of his hands cupping my face. "Yes."

"Yes?" I ask in a small voice. Incredulous that he'd just pick up his life in New York and move to Colorado.

"Yes, sunshine. I'll do it."

I grin up at him, feeling as though a weight has been lifted. I didn't realize I was so stressed about finding someone. I know

I've been putting it off, but that's just what I do, I put things off. But this feels good. Right. For him to work with me.

I'm glad I asked him.

I feel even better knowing that he'll be coming home with me. Maybe I need to trust myself, my emotions, and his and stop dragging my feet. There's been something between us for so long, I want to let it happen the way it's supposed to.

He smiles down at me and for a moment, I think he's going to kiss me. My heart flutters at the thought. But instead he releases my face and takes a step back. "Should we hit the pools and talk details?"

"Absolutely."

"I found this really fantastic space. It's on the corner of the main street in Estes Park and it's perfect," I tell him. He's still in the hot tub, and I'm on the edge with my feet dangling in. He's watching me attentively and only once has he glanced at my little sun tattoo. "I still don't have a name but I kind of want to name it something that is sort of a Taylor Swift reference, but that might be too much so I don't know."

"I'll start brainstorming ideas," Sam says. "What about your menu? Do you know what you want to do yet?"

"I've got a breakfast menu almost finished and I want to have a lunch menu. I'd really love for it to be a little cafe that's only open until two or three. I'm tired of working all night long, even though I haven't done that in months." Not since I left New York.

"You need your evenings to relax or hang out with friends, or to reread Emma." He smiles at me.

Or to kiss him, I think. I give him a smile. "How do you remember that?"

"Remember what?"

"That Emma is my favorite book."

He looks at me like he can't believe I just said that. "Oh I don't know, maybe it's the fact that you reread it at least once a year. Or maybe the fact that I stole a copy from you once and you never asked for it back and the next week I saw you reading another copy."

"I knew you stole it on purpose," I say.

"You never asked for it back." He shrugs. "So I kept it. It's the copy I read from that night in New York."

"Did you read all of it?" I ask. It's a dumb question because Sam is a reader. And he did start reading it out loud to me, something I've managed to forget though it wasn't that long ago.

"I've read it twice," Sam says, surprising me. "Though the first time, I didn't read much of the book, I just read all of your highlights and notes. I wanted to know what you loved about it."

I shake my head and laugh. "I was mad for about ten seconds when I realized you'd taken my annotated copy, but then I got to do it again and that was a lot of fun."

"Happy to have helped," Sam says.

My phone that's sitting on top of my cover-up lights up. I reach over to grab it.

"Noah and Tally and her family just landed in Los Angeles," I tell him. "They are going to get here so late."

"At least they have all day tomorrow to sleep, before the wedding on Friday."

"True."

"Noah's expecting me to stay in your room again tonight, since they don't land here until like two," he says.

"That's okay."

"Hopefully the AC is fixed. If it's not, I might sleep naked," he says and I blush.

"Uh," is all I manage to get out.

"I'm kidding. I just wanted to see how you'd react to that. You're adorable when you blush." He smiles and swims to where I'm sitting by the edge of the hot tub. Close enough to touch, but he doesn't reach out and close the gap between us. "And now I want to know what you're thinking."

Nope. No way am I going to tell him that for a split second, an image flashed into my head of all the things he and I could spend the night doing. We are married after all.

"I'm thinking that it's time to go jump in the pool." I stand and grab my clothes and shoes and phone before I head toward one of the pools. I drop my stuff on an empty chair and jump in without looking to see if he is behind me.

'Annie." I hear his voice as I come up out of the water. He's a foot away from me but not touching me.

He knows better than to touch me when I'm not expecting it.

"Sam," I say as I wipe water out of my eyes.

There's so much we need to talk about. About the future. About our marriage. But I move toward him in the water and his arms go around me. His hands on my hips. I warm my arms around his neck.

"What are we doing?" he asks in a voice that sounds oddly strangled.

"Having fun?" I say it like a question.

He shakes his head and goes to pull away, but I pull him closer.

"Kiss me," I whisper. He freezes. My mind is thrown back in time to the night before I left New York, when I asked him to kiss me, only this time, I'm different. He's different, and this time, I'm truly ready to kiss my husband and all that comes with it. I don't want to just have fun, I want the real deal. Even if the only person I'm ready to admit that to is myself.

"What?"

"Kiss me, Sam," I say again and this time, he does.

I'm so much shorter than him, but in the pool it doesn't really matter. It's nearly 9 p.m. and there aren't many people here. I close my eyes and melt into the kiss.

His lips are soft and slow and warm. It reminds me of the kiss he gave me at the courthouse the day we got married. Until it doesn't.

He deepens the kiss, pulling me closer to him, I wrap my legs around his waist, and and he sighs my name against my lips.

It nearly undoes me.

I break away from him, though our foreheads are still touching. "Sam," I whisper.

"Yes, sunshine?" His voice is deep and raspy.

"I think I'm ready for bed now."

He nods once, and then he's pulling away and hopping out of the pool. My heart dips to my belly as I watch him run a towel over his hair. I get out more slowly and he wraps my towel tightly around my shoulders. We don't talk as we head up to our room.

The door clicks shut behind us and I feel goosebumps cover my skin as the cold air from the AC hits me.

"I'm not ready for more than kissing." My voice shakes, but not from the cold. I don't want to disappoint him, but I'm not ready for more. Maybe someday, but I don't even know if that's possible. My therapist told me that with the right person, it will be someday. That being with someone who you truly love and care about will feel different than everything did with Mitch, who just took and took and took.

He gives me a look from across the room that is so soft and tender that my heart cracks wide open and I just want to give him the world. "Kissing you is my favorite thing."

I feel like the words should be sarcastic in some way,

because this is Sam, who tends to make a joke out of everything. But he's serious.

I nod. "I'm going to put dry clothes on."

"I'll be here." Sam gestures to the room.

My heart pounds in my chest. I don't know when I last felt this way, if I've ever felt this way. I feel nervous but excited. I'm not nervous about being with Sam or worried that he'll try something. I'm nervous about what all of this means and where we go from here. But tonight, I want to get out of my head and stop overthinking everything.

I change quickly before heading back out in the main room. He changed while I was in the bathroom and now he's wearing his gray sweats and a worn T-shirt from Estes Park. I wonder when he went there.

I pause awkwardly halfway between the bathroom and the couch where he is sitting. "Hi."

"Come here,'"he says in a reverent and awed voice as he holds out his hand to me.

I want to run to him, but I force myself to walk. I don't want to seem overeager. His hand wraps around mine and I fall against him on the couch. My legs go over his lap and he wraps an arm around me and I lay my head on his shoulder.

We're quiet for a moment as he holds me. The same way he held me that night he found me in the shower.

"I love the way you look at me," I say, breaking the silence.

"Yeah?" Sam asks. "And how exactly do I look at you?"

"Like I'm the only person in the world you can see. Like I'm the best thing in your life and you can't relax until you've found me in a room." Like he loves me.

Sam pulls me a little closer. "If I told you that you are the only person in the world that I want to see, would you believe me?"

I look up at him and our noses brush. Neither of us pull away. "Yes."

He closes the distance between us again and brushes his lips against mine. "I could spend forever kissing you."

His confession makes me warm all over as he deepens the kiss, pulling me fully onto his lap. I run my fingers through his long, curly hair and sigh as his fingers move up and down my back, his touch so light I should barely notice them but it's like he's set fire to all of my nerve endings.

As I lose myself to his kiss, I can't help but think that I could probably spend my life kissing him forever too.

At some point, the kissing slows and we fill the quiet with stories from the past six months. I tell him all about Hannah and how she's the friend I never expected but the one I needed. I tell him how I still haven't told my mom that I'm back in Colorado, because I don't know how to talk to her as an adult without her making me feel like I'm somehow used or broken because of what happened with Mitch.

I confess that I haven't been thrilled about coming to Maui for Noah's wedding, but that having Sam here makes it easier for me.

"It's been so hard to be without you in New York." He tells me quietly. "I quit YouTube."

This makes me sit up. "You what?"

"I'm done with the vlogging life." He pulls me back against him, our fingers threading together again. "It's time I settle down."

"Yeah?" I ask. I know he means with me, and for the first time, the thought doesn't make me want to run. I want it too.

"Yeah. And I didn't know you were in Colorado, but I was already planning on heading back out there until I figured things out. But now I'll be there, with you."

"I like the sound of that." I reach up and touch his beard. He kisses me again and I melt into him.

At some point, we move from the couch to the bed because I'm so exhausted I can barely keep my eyes open.

"How are you still so awake?" I ask. "It's like almost four in the morning in New York, doesn't your body feel it?" I'm feeling it, it's nearly two in the morning in Colorado.

I feel him press his lips against my hair. "Probably. But I've been wishing for this since I was seventeen, so I'm very awake."

I give him a squeeze and curl into him more. "I'm so glad I'm your husband," I say through a yawn. "I mean that you're my husband."

I feel his deep chuckle. "Well, wife, I think it's time for you to get some sleep."

He flips off the lamp and plunging us into darkness.

"And you're sure this is okay?" I ask. Even before Mitch, it seemed like all any guy ever wanted was to get in my bed and have their way with me, which is another reason why I stayed away from dating.

"This is more than okay, sunshine. If I died tomorrow, I would die a happy man."

"Please don't die," I say. I stop fighting to keep my eyes open.

"I'm not planning it," he murmurs. "Not anytime soon."

I lift myself up, which takes more effort than I realize it would because I'm so close to sleep, and I kiss his cheek.

"Goodnight, Sam."

"Goodnight, sunshine."

And then I fall asleep wrapped in my husband's arms.

32

—

SAM

The next morning I wake up bleary eyed to someone banging on our door. At some point in the night, I made my way to my own pillow, but Annie followed and she's curled against me. I could get used to waking up every morning like this, with her in my arms.

The banging on the door happens again, followed by a doorbell.

"Who in the world?" I groan into her hair.

"Maybe if we ignore them, they will just go away," she murmurs, curling closer to me.

The knocking doesn't stop. "Come on, open up!"

This time, Annie groans. It's Noah.

I feel trapped. Maybe this is what Monica and Chandler felt like the morning of Ross's wedding when they were together in Chandler's room and Ross came in. Except this isn't *Friends* and Noah knows that I slept in here. But he doesn't know that we spent the night cuddling, after kissing, before we fell asleep.

"He's going to see the couch is still a couch," I say as I untangle myself from Annie. She reaches for me.

"That's okay," she says, which surprises me because she is

the one who originally requested we not tell Noah yet. "I mean, we can just tell him the couch bed was broken and that we had to share a bed. I still think we should wait until after his wedding to tell him about us."

"I'm fine with that," I say as Noah knocks on the door again.

"What are you two doing in there?"

"Just a second!" I holler back, then look at Annie. "Can I kiss you again, before Noah is in here and I have to go back to pretending to love you from afar?"

"I might have gross morning breath." She ducks beneath the covers.

"That's alright, sunshine."

She peeks above the covers and nods yes and I press a quick kiss against her lips before she can pull me in. I run a hand through my sleep ruffled hair and move toward the door. "Showtime," I whisper right before I open the door.

Thankfully, Noah has always known of my not so secret feelings about Annie, so I don't have to pretend too much. But fighting the urge to not touch her might be difficult now that I can.

"About time," Noah says and then he appears in the room in front of me. "We just got here about an hour ago. Our flight was delayed again, so we just got checked in. Tally and her sister are sleeping, and I think her sister's boyfriend also said something about taking a nap, but I'm not sure we'll see much of him anyway because he doesn't really like people." Noah is rambling on and I keep waiting for him to notice how the sheets are rumpled and Annie looks as though she's been kissed. Or maybe only I can see that because I'm the one who made her look that way.

"So I just wanted to give you your key—" Noah looks into the room and looks back at me with daggers in his eyes. "Did you sleep with my sister? I told you she was off limits. I warned you, I didn't want either of you to get hurt."

"You don't know anything," Annie snaps from the bed. "We're both adults. We can take care of ourselves."

I jump in before Noah gets the wrong idea though, "The couch bed wouldn't come out, we only slept. Nothing more."

Noah glances between the two of us and decides to go after me instead of Annie, which I'm honestly grateful for. I don't know what I'd do if he said something even semi-mean to her. "If you put one finger on my sister..."

"I think you should think long and hard about what you're about to say next," I say, my voice is quiet but there's a threat underneath. "Because that woman right there might be your sister, but she's my..." I'm about to say wife, but Annie clears her throat behind us and we both look at her.

"You're what?" Noah asks me.

"I love her," I say quietly to him, even though I know that Annie can hear us. "And I just...don't talk like that about your sister. We're two consenting adults, so if something were to happen between us, it would be fine."

Noah blinks at me once. "I'm way too tired for this conversation. Here's the room key, but let me sleep for a few hours before you move your stuff in."

I take the key and nod at him.

"We're just two doors down." Then he leaves without another word.

I look at Annie, worried that she'll freak out on me for almost telling her brother. I didn't mean to, it just almost slipped out because it feels like the most normal and natural thing in the world to call her my wife. To have her as my wife.

"You almost called me your wife." Annie grins up at me.

"You're not mad?" I ask and she pats the bed beside her and shakes her head.

"Not at all. Now come back to bed, I was having a good time waking up in your arms and Noah ruined that."

She doesn't need to ask me twice. I'm in the bed next to her in a second, pulling her against me. "I could get used to this."

"Me too," Annie says. "Also, should we talk about how we're going to act in front of everyone at the wedding and before that?"

I bury my face in her neck, leaving a trail of kisses up to her chin before I kiss her on the lips. She melts into me and I grin against her mouth. "How about we just do this?"

"SAM!" She squeals, but she kisses me again. "I'm serious."

"So am I." I smirk at her and there's laughter in her eyes. "But, like I said the other day, whatever you want to do, it's up to you."

She relaxes against me and I'm relieved. It's hard to give up control, especially when all I want to do is yell out to the world that she's my wife and the love of my life and my best friend. But letting her decide how we announce things is the right move.

"I think we should just act normal."

I kiss her again. "This is pretty normal, sunshine."

It takes her several minutes to reply, and when she does, she's breathless. "I think the best plan for the next few days will to be acting like we're friends. Maybe a little flirting. But no kissing."

"Guess I'd better kiss you as much as I can now then, right?" I ask.

Annie laughs. "I'm all yours this morning."

When we finally get out of bed—hours later—I have a single text waiting for me from Chiara.

CHIARA

Just wanted to give an update about the Mitch case. They have enough to at least put him up for trial, possibly more to put him away for good. Along with new charges of money laundering. Annie won't have to testify unless she wants to.

Thanks for the update. I'll let Annie know, I'm with her in Maui.

Go take care of our girl.

Always.

I slide my phone back into my pocket as Annie comes back to the bed. I will tell her the news, eventually. Not today, probably not even in the next little bit. She deserves to know, but she also deserves to have some peace on this vacation.

After I tell her my feelings, we can have a conversation about everything that happened and she can decide if she wants to testify against Mitch or not. I'm happy to do it if I need to. But it should be up to her if she wants to or not.

"Hi." Annie slides into my arms and kisses my cheek.

"Hi." *I love you* is on the tip of my tongue, but I don't say it. I want to, but I don't want to rush her.

"Ready for all of this?" I assume she means her brother's wedding and all the parties that come with it.

"I am. It's about time Noah got his happy ending."

Annie gives me a hug before stepping out of my embrace. "It really is."

33

ANNIE

After everyone gets some rest, we spend the rest of the day with Noah and Tally and Tally's family. By late-afternoon, I'm feeling peopled out.

"Want to head upstairs for a little break before the bachelor and bachelorette parties?" Sam asks quietly as we're coming back from the pool. I don't know what Sam, Noah, Drew (Holly's fiancé), and Tally's dad are going to do, but it already feels like too much to hangout with Tally, Gran, Holly, and Beth, even though they are all pretty great. Plus, my mom will be there.

"Yes," I say even though I know it isn't possible. The party starts in less than an hour, that's hardly enough time to get a breather.

"Let's go," he says. He murmurs something to Noah then leads me to the elevator. I'm silent on the ride up to our room, too exhausted to even think.

When we get to the room, Sam guides me to the bed. "I'm really not—" I start to say that I'm not in the mood for anything but Sam cuts me off.

"I didn't bring you up here to try to pull a move on you," he says as he stands behind me. His hands fall lightly on my shoulders as his thumbs start to rub the knots in my neck. "Is this okay? I promise to only touch you here. You've seemed so tense, and I just want to help you relax if I can."

I'm moved to tears by his promise. I want to say that this is hard for me, letting him in like this, trusting a man to touch me, but I don't even have to say the words because Sam already knows.

His hands stop and leave my neck. 'I need a verbal yes before I do anymore."

"Yes," I say, hoping he can't hear the emotion in my voice.

If he does, he doesn't say anything about it as he lays his hands back on me and begins to knead out the knots in my neck. I feel myself relax as he does so.

I've always been introverted, preferring my books to people. Or a kitchen to people. My brother knows this. Sam knows this. But I promised myself I would put on my best show and do anything that Noah asked, because he's my brother and he's getting married. And knowing him, he'll only ever get married once. It's still all exhausting though.

"I am not excited to spend two hours with my mother," I finally admit. Mom's flight got in this afternoon, and she and her new boyfriend have been 'resting' so they could be ready for the parties tonight and wedding ceremony tomorrow.

"Is she still mad about everything that happened in New York?" Sam asks as his thumb works on a particularly tight spot.

I nod. "She was mad that I went there in the first place. She's mad I don't talk to her more. And she blames me for not being a better judge of character and for dating someone I worked with, as if that was the problem."

"Did you tell her what happened?" Sam asks.

"A bit. Noah filled her in on the rest. But she still blames me. My therapist said it's probably her way of projecting because she hates that she's never been great at picking men to date, but it still sucks. Mom is amazing at victim shaming."

"I'm sorry, Annie," Sam says softly.

"It's not your fault."

"I wish I could go to the party with you, give her someone else to talk to."

"Hopefully, she'll be interested in Tally more than me so she won't hyper-focus on the fact that I'm not getting married at the ripe old age of twenty-eight."

I can practically hear Sam smirking.

"I am not going to tell her that I am married though, she'll throw a huge fit about it, even if it is what she wants."

"You could always tell her we started seeing each other, if she asks about your dating status," Sam suggests.

"I know." I sigh. "There are just more interesting things to talk about than whether or not I've found a man to settle down with. I would love to tell her about my restaurant, but she'd only laugh and tell me I need to get a real job. Or a husband who makes all the money. She can't see how hypocritical it is given how many men she's dated—yet never marries—but she still expects me to want to get married."

I feel his hands tense. "I don't want to make you do something you don't want to do."

I reach up and touch his hand. "I know." I turn to look at him, my shoulder brushing his chest as we stare at each other. "You aren't, you haven't. I really do want to see where this goes. I know I haven't said that yet, but I would like to give this a chance. I think I just don't want the reason I get married to be because my mom wanted that for me."

"Well, it's a good thing that you got married for me to have your insurance instead then, right?" He gives me a half smile, like he's ready to keep making jokes so I smile, but he'll stop if they don't land.

"Exactly," I say. "Now can you work on the knot on the left side? That one has been killing me for weeks."

"Of course." His hands are warm and the pressure on the knots feels good. I let myself fully relax, something I rarely do, but I trust him and that's huge.

I don't think about how in an hour I'll have to spend time with my mom and I don't let myself worry about what will happen with me and Sam once we get to Colorado. In this moment, I'm just letting myself enjoy this.

And for a few minutes, I get to feel like myself, something I haven't felt in a really long time.

Far too soon, it's time for the bachelorette party. I love Tally—she's perfect for my brother—but I've hit my people limit for the day, and I don't know how I'll be able to pretend that I'm fully fine around everyone.

"You can do this, sunshine," Sam whispers before he presses a kiss against my forehead. The elevator chime dings, signaling it's time to get on and head downstairs and go our separate ways. The guys are going to a restaurant for dinner and soda—since none of them drink these days—and the girls are going to the resort's spa, which Tally's grandmother rented out for us tonight. I also hope there's food because I'm already feeling hungry.

"I don't know if I can," I say as we step onto the elevator.

"Just stick with Tally or her sister, you don't even have to talk to your mom if you don't want to," he says.

I want to believe him. I hope that she'll be on her best behavior, but I'm mentally preparing myself and I'm already exhausted. "I'm going to need a week-long nap when we get home."

He smiles. "Anything you need. Anything you want."

I give his hand three squeezes. "Thank you for caring so much."

"Always," he says as the elevator reaches the ground floor. I look at him in wonder. How did I get so lucky that he cares for me so deeply? He lets go of my hand before we see anyone. He's letting me take charge of when I want anyone to know about us, and right before my brother's wedding? Probably not the best time.

We're all meeting out by the pool and I hear the group before I see them. Mom's laugh is loud and I'm already cringing. We turn the corner and I see them, all standing in a group. We're the last to arrive.

Mom breaks away from her conversation with Noah and approaches Sam and I.

"Noah told me the two of you would be coming down together, but I told him I wouldn't believe it until I saw it for myself." Mom gives Sam a hug first, something that I'm not surprised by, but it still stings. Then she reaches for me. "My darling girl!"

Mom always goes over the top the first few minutes we always see each other. I don't know if it's because she feels guilty that we haven't talked in ages, or if she really wants to try harder this time. But I know her praise will only last so long, before she'll find something to criticize.

"You look good," Mom says as she pulls back. "Less stressed, which is good. I was worried you were going to get too many wrinkles. You're young, you need to relax and take care of your face."

And there it is. "Thanks Mom." It's easier to just pretend that her comments don't sting than to confront her and make a scene in front of everyone. I feel Sam stiffen beside me, and his hand on my lower back presses against me and I lean into it.

Mom might not ever see me as worthy, but at least I know that Sam does.

No one seems to notice us touching, not even Mom, which is good. I'm too tired for any explanations tonight.

"At least you can get a facial tonight, that ought to help. Are you still working in that restaurant?"

"I'm sure the facial will be great," I say through tight lips, but before I can answer the question about work, Noah claps his hands.

"Alright, time to party!" It's weird to see my normally quiet brother acting so excited about being social. But he is finally marrying Tally, and I guess that is a big part of it.

"That's my boyfriend," Mom whispers to me, not hiding her obvious point. The man, only a handful of years older than me, gives her a huge grin.

I swear I throw up in my mouth a little.

"Cool," I somehow manage to say. Gross is what I really mean, but I'd never tell my mother that.

"Have fun," Sam whispers to me, before giving my hand a quick, discreet squeeze before leaving my side.

"You too," I say. He heads over to where my brother and Drew are standing near Tally's dad.

"Hello, dear," Gran, Tally's grandmother, says before she wraps me in a big hug. I've always liked Gran. Her hugs feel like a warm blanket and I want to melt into it. The woman oozes love and goodness and all things that my mother has never been. I met her last year, at Thanksgiving, when Noah proposed to Tally.

"Hi, Gran." I return her hug. "Have you met my mom?"

"I just met her. Noah introduced us." Gran gives me a smile that tells me she'll be on my side if it comes down to it.

"Great," I say.

"Well, have fun with your facials and getting your nails done," Noah tells all of us. "We're going to go eat food."

I try not to think about all the good food I'll be missing while someone does my nails. I can't even remember the last time I got my nails done. But Tally wanted to treat everyone for the wedding.

"See you tomorrow!" Tally hugs Noah before letting him go. He pulls her in for a quick kiss that leaves her beaming. After this, they won't see each other until the wedding tomorrow. Noah's a purist in every wedding tradition out there. Though, I am surprised that he didn't bring his dog Mo with him. He never goes anywhere without that dog. I can't imagine this resort allows animals, so that's probably why.

When we get to the spa, Mom sits right next to me. "You've put on a little weight, are you eating too much of your food?"

I ignore her whisper because it's better to simply ignore her than engage in any conversation. Talking with my mother has never been productive. Thankfully, therapy showed me that it's okay to set boundaries. And one thing I won't talk to my mother about is my weight or eating or food.

"Oh, so you moved to New York and have barely said a word to me in ten years and you are still going to ignore me?"

"I'm happy to talk to you, mom," I tell her, "just not about food. Or my weight, which is perfectly healthy by the way."

She grunts, "Fine. Would you like to hear about my boyfriend?"

We're still waiting on everyone to change into their robes so we've got ample time to fill. I wish there was something to eat, at least that would sort of distract me.

"Sure," I say, even though I have no desire to learn about the man that's been hanging out with my mother.

"I met him at the grocery store, can you believe it? I can't believe he's single. He's so charming and his family comes from so much money." Mom sighs like this is the best trait a man could possibly have, being rich. "He's thirty-two, so I know he's young, but wow is he amazing in bed..."

I hold up a hand, "I'm going to have to stop you right there," and thankfully, mom doesn't say another word because everyone else comes out of the dressing room and we all shuffle down the hallway to the massage tables. I pick the one furthest from my mother, and slowly feel the tension drain from my shoulders as I get a massage.

"Are you ready to marry my brother?" I ask Tally after our massages are finished and we're getting our nails done. Lucky for me, Mom's stylist is sitting on the other side of the room so she only has Gran to talk to.

Tally gets a dreamy look in her eyes. "Sure am."

"He's been waiting for this moment for years. Since the first time you met," I say.

Holly snorts. "She'll never admit it, but so was she."

"I'll admit it," Tally says. "The first time I saw him I imagined a whole life with him. Which sounds a little nuts, and it probably was. But I was eighteen and have you seen him? He's gorgeous."

"I mean, he's my brother so I don't think he's gorgeous."

Holly and Tally laugh with me.

"Do you think you'll ever get married?" Holly asks me. She's got a shiny ring on her left hand, a new addition Noah said.

"I always thought I wouldn't," I say honestly. "But lately, I don't know. Maybe."

Is this a lie? I'm already married, at least legally. But I have been thinking about what a marriage a life with Sam would actually look like. And I don't hate what I'm imagining.

"Ooo, are there any men you're interested in?" Holly asks. I laugh.

"Sorry about her, she's a little love-sick right now. She just got engaged last week," Tally tells me.

"It's okay," I say. "And yeah, there is one guy. He's my best friend."

Holly puts her hand on her heart like I've just said the most romantic thing in the world. "That's so sweet!"

I smile, unsure of what else to say. While I do like Sam—I love him, if we're being technical about it—but there's still so much we need to work through, that I need to work through. I just hope he'll keep being patient with me and sticking with me even if it takes awhile for me to fully embrace the life he wants. The life I want now too.

I'm not sure when it changed. When I went from swearing off marriage to picturing what our future house will be like. But somewhere along the way with Sam, it changed. I changed. And now I want something more.

I'm exhausted by the time I get back to my room. I hate that I'm disappointed when I find it empty. I turn on the TV, just so I don't have to be alone with my thoughts. All I want to do is curl up in bed and not see my mother for another six months to a year, but I have to see her tomorrow, and I'm already dreading it.

I find *The Office* playing on one of the channels and let it play while I change into my pajamas. My face feels fresh and clean after my facial and I'm not sure what to do. I know Sam was going to stay with Noah tonight, duties of the best man and all, but I hate feeling alone.

My phone vibrates on the nightstand and I reach for it slowly. My heart beats faster when I see Sam's name.

SAM

You up still? Or back yet? I have some food for you.

My stomach grumbles in response. I text him back.

I'm up. And I'm starving.

The door swings open a few seconds later. He walks in with the room key in one hand and a bag of food in the other. I have to restrain myself from jumping up too quickly. Sam came to see me! I don't hug him, instead I move to the small table in the corner and watch as he starts to unload the contents of the bag.

"I got you some nachos and a burger, because this was probably the best burger I've ever had and I needed you to try it and I know you love nachos."

I nod greedily. "Nachos are the food I'd like to have as my last meal."

"That's a tad bit morbid," he says.

I shrug as I pull off the lid and am hit with the smell of melted cheese and spicy salsa. "But it's true."

He laughs, and my belly flips. All of this feels so normal, I just hope it will stay that way.

34

SAM

Watching Annie try new food is one of my favorite things in the world. Most people I know eat mainly because they have to, because we need to eat in order to survive. But Annie? She seems to savor each bite. It's like watching a kid see snow for the first time when she's eating good food.

It's simply magical. I hadn't exactly forgotten that, but I've been hyper-aware of it since we've been here in Maui.

I also am aware that watching someone else eat is a bit weird, so I look out the dark window instead.

"I realized something about my mom tonight," she says and I turn back to her as she puts another chip in her mouth.

"Oh yeah?" I ask, curious to see what she's learned about her mom.

Annie nods. "I realized that I'll never be like her. She continues to date men, one after the other and she always has. I always avoided relationships because I was so worried I'd be like her. But I'm not like her, because she hates being alone."

I nod, not quite understanding where Annie is going with this.

"Ever since Dad left, I don't think she's been single for more than a week. And Dad left when I was six. That's twenty-two years of horrible relationships all because she doesn't love herself. But I'm not that way. I'm comfortable in my skin—mostly anyway—I'm learning to love myself again and let myself be loved." She looks up at me as she says these words and I reach across the table and take her hand in mine.

"I've still got a lot to work through, but I'm not my mom," she says and then she grins. "So maybe the marriage thing will work out for us. If we can move slowly."

"I hope so," I tell her. I could have told her a long time ago that she's nothing like the woman who raised her. That she's kind and gentle and loving in a way her mother never will be. "And we can move as slow as you need."

"Thanks, and I hope so too."

"Call me if you need anything tonight." I don't want to leave. Now that we've agreed to be whatever this is—dating and already married—I don't want to leave her side, especially after the conversation we just had about her mom and what she realized. But I already promised I'd stay with Noah tonight. Plus, he doesn't know about us yet.

"I'll be fine," Annie promises, but her voice is tight, like it always is after she spends any time with her mom. "I've got a book." I glance at the nightstand and see her worn copy of Emma sitting there.

"I should have brought my copy," I say.

She laughs, a sound that eases some of the anxiety I feel about leaving her alone tonight.

"What is it about you and that book?" she asks.

"I could ask you the same thing," I shoot back and look at

her. Her eyes have that familiar gleam in them, the one that always means that teasing is coming.

"You really have liked me for so long," she says, her voice soft and in a quiet awe—like she's finally just letting this realization sink in.

I take a step toward her and sit in the empty chair as she eats her nachos.

"You have no idea," I tell her. I've told her the truth, for the most part, but it's still terrifying to have my confession out in the open.

There's a moment of silence. "Thanks for the food," Annie says. "I really was starving. They didn't give us any food to eat at the spa, saying something about how we need to watch what we eat right before the wedding. What a load of garbage. People need to eat."

"I mean, to be fair, you did have a little food before you went to the spa."

She swats her hand at me. "A granola bar does not count as dinner."

I see the pale pink of her nails. "You got your nails done."

Annie closes her fist and puts her hands under the table. "I don't think they've had any sort of polish or gel on them since I was in high school."

"They look nice," I say. She has always been self conscious of her hands. She said she couldn't ever paint her nails because she had too many freckles and adding another color would just draw more attention. I can't remember now if she told me that before or after she dated Mitch, but it must have been after, when she started to lose her sparkle. When she dimmed herself because for some reason she thinks a dimmed version of herself is better than just being her. I want to show her how much I love her, her whole self. That she can do anything she wants and I'll always love her.

"Just call if you need anything," I say again.

"I will." She smiles at me. It's soft and sweet and I just want to melt in it. But I also know that if I kiss her now, I won't want to stop. So I stay where I'm standing across the table.

"Well, I should get back. Noah said we're going to watch a movie or something before bed and I told him I wouldn't be long."

"Have fun," Annie says. "And really, thanks for the food."

"Anytime," I say. She stands and wraps her arms around me. "I'm really glad you're here."

An ache that's been in my body since Annie left New York disappears as I wrap my arms around her and hold her against me. Like I've been holding onto it, waiting for her to run, but instead she's coming to me. I never want to move.

But slowly, I let her go and step back. "I'll see you in the morning, unless you need anything."

"I'll see you tomorrow Sam." She squeezes my hand and follows me to the door.

I want to say more, but I don't. Instead I leave and head down the hall to her brother's room.

The new action movie ends and Noah falls asleep almost immediately after the lights go out. I flip my phone over and over in my hand, waiting for a text from Annie, but in my gut I know that she's not going to text me. She doesn't ever want to seem weak, because her mom would say something about it. She always acts so strong, even when she doesn't have to.

But I still want her to need me. I feel like she needs me tonight, but I don't want to seem protective and overbearing, so I'll wait for her to need me. As if reading my mind, a text comes through and my phone vibrates.

ANNIE

Help

The one word has me up in a split second. I'm pulling on a T-shirt and am sprinting down the hall before I realize I'm not wearing any shoes. But it doesn't matter. I scramble out a text to Noah, telling him Annie needed something—at least that's what I hope I sent—before I use the key to her room to enter.

I find Annie curled up in the middle of the bed, her arms are wrapped tightly around her legs and she's got that hollow stare she had when I found her in the shower, fully clothed, all those months ago.

My heart seems to stop and time slows. What happened to make her this way this time? Last time, she didn't talk for hours after I got her changed and into bed. But that time she'd seen Mitch. The TV is still playing quietly on the dresser, like it was when I brought her food. The food has been cleaned up and her hair is ruffled like it is after she sleeps.

I move to her, my arms coming around her and she shudders.

"You came." Her words are barely a whisper.

"Of course," I breathe back.

Then, she falls apart and I hold her while she cries.

It might be minutes or hours later, when Annie shifts in my lap to look up at me. Her eyes are red and exhausted.

"Hi," I say, it's becoming a thing between us—greeting each other while we're already together—and I like it.

"Hi," Annie says.

"You okay?" I ask, even though it feels like a stupid question to pose because obviously she isn't doing okay.

"Better now," she says softly. I want so badly to ask her what's going on in her head but I don't want to push if she doesn't want to talk. "I fell asleep and had a nightmare. I felt like I couldn't breathe when I woke up so I texted."

"I'm glad you texted." I give her a squeeze, pulling her closer to me. "Do you want to talk about your nightmare?"

She shakes her head.

"Okay."

"I mean…" Annie sighs. "I want to, but it isn't your burden to carry. I don't want to put all of this on you, Sam."

Her voice isn't full of its usual confidence. She sounds timid, worried about what I might say or do if she dumps this on me. But it wouldn't be dumping. I'll happily carry this for her.

"You can tell me."

She is quiet for a long moment. "It's always the same dream. I'm always somewhere with Mom and then Mitch appears and they both start talking. At first to each other and then to me. It's not bad at first, some comments that sting a little like how they don't like my dress or hair or something, but then it gets worse."

She closes her eyes and I reach over and lace her fingers through mine, letting her know that I'm here once she's ready to tell me more.

"Then all I can hear is Mitch yelling the vile things he used to say all the time and Mom is cheering him on, like she's proud of him. It makes me sick every time. I know she probably wouldn't do that in real life, but the way her words make me feel sometimes are the same feelings I get after these dreams, nightmares. Whatever."

"Have you talked to someone about this?" I know she mentioned a therapist, but I don't know how any of that works beyond what she's told me.

She shakes her head. "They don't happen often enough for me to feel like I should talk about them." There she goes again, trying not to burden others and keep all her pain to herself.

"But they happen," I say gently. "I am happy to listen, but

I'm not a therapist and can't give you the tools you need to work through this. Will you talk to your therapist about this when we get home?"

She nods against my chest and I think she's started to cry again.

"What can I do?" I ask, feeling helpless. I wish there was more I could help her with. I wish I could take away every bad feeling and thought she's having right now.

"Stay with me," Annie says softly. As if I was ever going to leave.

"Of course." I pull us against the pillows and wrap the comforter around us. A tiny cocoon just for the two of us.

Eventually, her breathing slows and she relaxes in my arms. Only then am I able to also fall asleep.

35

ANNIE

I wake up wrapped in the warmth that is Sam's arms. My back is against his chest and I can feel his steady breathing against me. I feel calm, which is a foreign feeling to me. Especially after having a PTSD episode like I did last night, I never wake up in the morning feeling calm. But having Sam's arms around me all night must have made a difference.

I'm starting to notice that having him around in general makes a difference. But it also makes me wary. I can't rely on him—or anyone—to help with my feelings. No one is ever that constant, and it isn't fair to put this on anyone else. I have to figure out how to feel calm and okay without the help of anyone else.

He lets out a long breath and I decide that for right now, just today, I'll let myself feel okay and safe in his arms. And tomorrow I'll start to figure out how to do this without him. He might be coming to Colorado with me, but I still won't make him ever carry the weight of my own mental illness.

That's too much to put on another person, even if we are married and going to see how it goes.

I feel him shift and I know he's awake, but sleepy. His arms tighten around me and pull me closer to his warm body. I wait for my body to stiffen, to tense, but I simply curl into him.

"Morning," he whispers against my hair. He moves and his lips skim the side of my neck and I lean into him even more. "I like waking up with you in my arms."

"I like it too."

He kisses my neck again and groans, not a happy one. "I should probably get back up to Noah, best man duties before the wedding and all. But I'd rather stay here with you all day."

"You can go be with Noah," I tell him, surprised that I actually mean the words. "And we can spend a day just like this once we get back to my little cabin in Colorado."

I feel his smile as he presses another feather light kiss against my skin before he slowly releases me. "I'll be counting down the days."

"Me too," I say, feeling suddenly shy. This man is my husband, I just promised him a day together in bed, what I've implied—intentional or not—is huge.

He knows me too well though. "We can do whatever you want that day. No expectations, just you and me, together."

I nod, though I feel guilty. Sam is a man, surely he has expectations. Mitch always did.

He reaches for me, pulling me into an awkward kneeling hug in the middle of the bed.

"I can feel you overthinking it," Sam tells me. "I know what you meant when you suggested a day together. I don't expect anything more than what we've already done to happen. I'm amazed and grateful that you even want that with me. I could spend the whole day with you reading beside me and I'd be the happiest man alive."

My eyes fill with tears. I want to believe him. But I know how relationships work. The guy is always so sweet and romantic and makes promises like he just made, but as the relationship goes on, men give up on being nice. They drop the romantic things and the only thing that is left is the expectation for more than the woman is often able to give.

I don't want our relationship to lose this magic, the bubble we're in here in Hawaii has been amazing, but real life isn't like that.

"Okay?" he asks when I don't respond.

"Okay," I say, maybe I can pretend for a little longer.

Sam gives my hand three squeezes before letting me go. "I'll see you soon?"

I nod in response. I'll need to head up to Tally's room in a bit, as a bridesmaid I get to get ready with her and her sister. Thankfully, I won't have to see or interact with Mom until after the ceremony.

Sam smiles at me and I forget my worries and let myself melt a little. I've always wanted to have a guy look at me like that and now he is looking at me like that.

I feel myself smile back and that seems to be enough for him to feel like I'm okay. He gives me a nod and heads out the door. I fall back onto the pillows, wondering if my head and my heart will ever be able to let myself fully fall for Sam. I love him, but it's still hard.

Tally went for casual beach wedding attire. I'm in my simple yellow sundress that I wore when Sam and I got married—the only dress I own—and I watch myself in the mirror as Tally's grandmother curls my hair.

"I noticed that Sam hasn't been able to keep his eyes off of you," Gran tells me. "You should give that boy a real chance. He loves you."

If she only knew the half of it.

"Gran!" Tally calls from across the room. "No matchmaking!"

Gran rolls her eyes in the mirror and I smile as she catches my eye.

Holly is also wearing a simple green pastel sundress and her hair is pinned up. The boys will be in tan slacks and white shirts with pastel ties. I don't know if I've ever seen Sam in a tie. He wore a nice T-shirt when we got married. He and I both don't really do fancy things.

Before I know it, it's time for the ceremony. The venue looks even better than when we saw it the other day. Holly and her fiancé Drew will walk down the aisle before Sam and I.

Tally is waiting inside the resort, so Noah and Sam approach me at the same time.

"You look like a million bucks," I tell my brother. He's in the same tan slacks as the groomsmen but his shirt has long sleeves.

"You too, sis," he gives me a hug and then looks at Sam. "Good thing Tally wanted to keep the wedding small and none of her cousins will be here. I'd have made one of them walk Annie down the aisle."

Sam frowns. "Over my dead body would I have let another man touch my wife."

My eyes go wide at his slip and I watch as Noah's eyes narrow at him. "Your what?"

Sam glances at me. "My wife."

Noah whirls to me. "You married him? Why would you do that? When did you do that? You're both going to end up with broken hearts."

"It's a long story," I tell Noah. "We can talk about it later. Right now, though, it's your moment."

Noah nods, once, jaw tight, but he turns to answer a question Tally's dad has.

"I'm sorry," Sam says. "That just kind of slipped out."

"I know. It's okay, it was going to come out at some point." I put my hand on Sam's hand. "You look nice too," and when he turns to look at me, it's like everyone else disappears and it's just us.

He grins at me. "You're stunning."

I hear Noah clear his throat, but neither of us look at him.

"Alright, how about we get this wedding started," Noah says. I know he's nervous, but the kind of nervous excited you feel before something good happens.

Sam lets go of my hands. "Let's get you married, brother." He claps Noah on the back.

Noah nods once before heading up the aisle. There are a handful of guests on the chairs set out, but most of us here are in the wedding party. Mom is making out with her boyfriend when I look at her so I look away. That's too weird and gross.

"I'm gonna need you to wear that dress for the rest of time," Sam says as the music starts. I glance up at him.

"I'm pretty sure it won't last forever."

"Well, for as long as it lasts then. Yellow is your color. You wore that when we got married and it about killed me."

I go warm all over. "I like your tie." I look up at Sam, he's got his hair pulled up in a bun on the top of his head and his beard is trimmed and neat. He looks nice all dressed up. Maybe we should dress up more often.

He smiles. "I like that we match."

"It's a wedding, of course we match," I whisper to him as Holly and Drew start up the aisle. We're right behind them.

"Well, I like it," Sam says. "We should get matching swimsuits for next year."

I nearly roll my eyes, but we're up and all eyes are on us. He holds out his arm and I slide my arm in his. "And we'll have to get us some rings."

My chest tightens slightly at the thought of this being a real marriage, but then I remember my promise to myself this morning. I can lose myself to this fantasy for a little longer. At least while we're here.

So I smile up at him, "Of course." But I won't let myself think too much about the future, that always leads to heartache. I can't put all of my problems on him.

At the end of the aisle, he reluctantly lets go of me, giving me a smile as we walk to either side of Noah.

Watching Tally's father lead her up the aisle doesn't give me the ache in my chest that I often get when I'm at weddings. Maybe it's because I'm already married and our ceremony was uncomplicated and to help Sam get insurance. I didn't have to worry about my dad not being there. I watch Noah as he takes Tally's hands, and his entire face is lit up. He's been hoping for this day for so many years.

I glance up behind him and find Sam watching me. I love the way he looks at me, as if there isn't anything or anyone else he'd rather be looking at. The view of the ocean is incredible from where we're standing and his best friend is getting married, and here he is, looking at me.

I feel the pull to glance away, but I fight it and hold his gaze. When Sam smiles at me, it's not a smirk or like he's got some secret intention that he's thinking about later. He's smiling at me like he really feels as though he's the luckiest man in the world to have me looking back at him.

It's that look that makes me know I'm a complete goner.

I'm in love with Sam Holland and I have been for a very long time. It's time to stop denying it and let myself completely fall.

36

ANNIE

After the ceremony, Noah catches my eye and I know it's time. Sam follows me over to where my brother is standing.

"I hope he doesn't think we were trying to upstage his wedding day," I tell Sam.

"He won't, he's a hopeless romantic. Hopefully we can explain to him everything and he'll just be happy for us," Sam says as he places his hand on the small of my back. "We never wanted to outshine his day, I can explain since he only knows right now because of me. It's going to be fine."

"I can talk. He's more mad that I'm going to break your heart than anything and I'm not sure how I feel about it. I mean, I guess I'm happy he's not trying to defend my honor or something, but it seems like he cares more about your feelings than mine."

We make it to Noah before Sam has a chance to reply.

"When did the two of you start dating?" Noah asks without saying hello. His arms are folded across his chest and his jaw is set. He looks like he's about to go to battle.

"Um," I say, unsure of how exactly to answer that. Dating? We kind of only started that this trip, but the answer could also be months ago or years ago. It's always been Sam, I just didn't realize it until recently.

"Technically," Sam says, answering for me. "Two days ago."

Noah's look is murderous. "And you had a shotgun wedding last night?"

"No," I say calmly. "We got married nine and a half months ago in New York."

"You what?" Noah asks, as if this explanation is worse than the two of us getting married last night or two days ago.

There's no easy way to say any of this. Noah has always been a straight laced kind of guy. Everything is black and white to him, which I get. But nothing about mine and Sam's marriage is black and white.

"Was it because of...." he starts to ask but Sam holds up a hand.

"You don't have to say his name, and no. It was because of my back."

Noah looks confused.

I jump in to explain. "Sam needed surgery, but he didn't have any health insurance so we got married because my insurance at the restaurant was fantastic."

"So you committed insurance fraud?" Noah's eyes grow wide.

"No," I answer. "Our marriage is real. You know how I've felt about marriage and Sam wasn't ready to settle down any time soon with anyone else. So we got married and got him on the insurance."

"And then what?" Noah asks looking between the two of us. "Have you been sleeping with other women while also sleeping with my sister?"

Sam moves and I put an arm out to stop him. "Noah," I warn, looking at my brother. But Sam steps in front of me, looking like he might punch his best friend.

"Is that really how little you think of me? That I am just this guy who travels the world and sleeps with as many women as possible?" Sam doesn't give Noah a chance to answer. "I've never even slept with anyone, not like that. You assumed and I never corrected you because I've been in love with Annie since I was seventeen and *you* were the one who told me to back off, to date other people so I wouldn't get hurt. But I love Annie."

Noah is gaping at us, speechless after the bomb Sam dropped on him. As if Sam's feelings haven't always been obvious. But to be fair, I didn't always see them.

"I'm sorry we didn't tell you the truth," Sam continues. "At first it was because you were so adamant that I never date your sister so I became who I thought you wanted to see. If I was never going to be worthy enough in your eyes, then what was the point of trying to change your mind?"

I squeeze Sam's hand, I'm in this with him. Because I love him too.

"And you're okay with marrying him?"

"Yes," I tell Noah. I haven't exactly told Sam that I love him yet, I'm not about to tell my brother first.

Sam starts talking before I can say anything else. "And then when she went to Colorado, it took everything in me not to chase after her, but I knew she needed space. But by then, she was my wife, and I was willing to wait as long as it took."

"Wait, back up." Noah says and both of us again and then stares at me. "When did you go to Colorado?"

I take a deep breath.

"I think it's time you and I had a little talk, older brother." I step toward Noah, and then look back at Sam "We'll meet up with you later?"

"Always." Sam smiles at me and Noah, and I walk toward the beach.

"Do you want the ring back?" Noah asks as we walk down

the beach, away from Sam.

It takes me a second to remember what he's talking about, then I laugh. "No thank you." Last Thanksgiving, I flew to Utah to give Noah our grandmother's ring that she left me in her will. Sam and I were already married then, but I didn't want that ring. It was always meant to be Tally and Noah's. Not mine.

"Wait, were the two of you already married when you brought it out for me to propose?" Noah asks me.

I nod. "We were. But it never was supposed to be anything real, at least not at first. I don't need that ring, it's much more Tally's taste than it is mine anyway. I feel like Grandma Marsha knew I'd give it to her somehow." Sam and I can find something simple that fits me better anyway.

Noah seems to relax a little. "So tell me what happened, start at the beginning."

And so I do. I tell him how Sam started spending more time in the city, because he was worried about me, and then about the accident.

"He was in so much pain, but assuring me he was saving for surgery," I tell Noah.

Noah laughs. "Sam has never been good with his own money. Not because he spends it on himself, but he's always giving it away." Noah stops in his tracks. "I can't believe he let me think he was such a playboy."

"That's Sam for you," I say. "Anyway, I offered to marry him so he could get on my insurance and get the surgery so he wouldn't be in so much pain. We fought about it for less than an hour because he was in so much pain. He looked me in the eye and said 'okay sunshine, let's do this.'"

"I should have known that he gave you a nickname because of how much he's always liked you," Noah says.

"I think neither of us really wanted to admit our feelings to each other, because of how I've always said I'd never get married. But the next day we went to the courthouse and by that evening we were married."

I leave out the part of the story where he kissed me at the courthouse and something happened inside of me that I ignored.

"After his surgery, I worked less to help him recover."

I feel tense as I get closer to the part of the story where I saw Mitch.

"Just after I got home from Thanksgiving with you and Tally, I ran into Mitch at work."

"You don't have to tell me, if you don't want," Noah offers.

"I'm okay," I say. I am mostly okay now. "He was keeping tabs on me, since he wasn't at the restaurant often and had seen the change on my insurance policy a few months before and he was livid that I hadn't told him I was getting married."

I shudder, trying to block out the memory of him yelling all the vile things he'd said, how after so much time, he could still make me feel so small.

"I don't remember leaving or heading home. All I know is that hours later, Sam returned from dinner with friends to find me soaking wet and freezing cold in the shower with all of my clothes still on. He helped me change and get warm. When I woke up in the middle of the night, he was still there."

"I'm glad he was there," he says. "I wish I could have been there."

"It's okay. Sam was there," I assure him, grateful for the thousandth time that Sam had been there. "Two days later, I went to Colorado. Emily had told me about this therapy type camp and I went to check it out."

"In the middle of winter?" Noah asks me.

"Well, it was the off season, but I did meet the owner, Hannah, randomly on my first day there, without realizing it was her. We're very good friends now. And I got a therapist. I'll be heading back there after the wedding and Sam is going to come with me. He's going to help manage my own cafe."

"Your own cafe? Annie, that's great!" Noah gives me a hug. "And is it bad to say that I'm glad you're out of New York?"

I smile. "Not bad at all. It was time to start somewhere new."

"And now?" Noah asks, "With Sam? That's real?"

My stomach flips. "I think so. I hope so. We'll see what happens. I still feel a tiny bit wary about marriage and a life with someone, but I'm in therapy and she's helping me work through a lot of the lies I believed growing up because of things Mom said and did. I think we're going to be okay, me and Sam."

"You really married my best friend and did't tell me for nine months?" Noah asks.

"I really did. I just didn't think it was going to last, so I wasn't supposed to ever have a reason to tell you." Looking back though, I should have known from the start that Sam and I were destined to stay together.

Noah looks out at the ocean.

"Are you mad?" I ask.

He runs a hand through his hair. "No. Yes. I don't know. It's kind of a big bomb, I need to process it. You gonna tell Mom?"

"I don't know yet. We might wait a little while to drop that news on her, so she can just enjoy your day. I don't want to take any of your spotlight. You and Tally deserve the best."

Noah nods. "Alright. I can be there if you need me to be when you tell her."

"I haven't even told her I've been in the mountains of Colorado for the past six months, so maybe someday." It's never been easy for me to talk to my mom. One step at a time though.

"Like I said, give me a call. Or just take Sam with you. The woman loves him."

I grin. "She really does. Did you know her new boyfriend is

only two years older than you and him? She was bragging about it to Gran last night, and Gran was a good sport about it, but I think she agrees with me that it's weird."

"Gross." Noah shudders. "Good thing you married Sam when you did, or she might go for him."

"Gross is right," I say. "Are you glad that you invited her to the wedding?"

Noah nods again. "Well, even with her dysfunctional relationships, she's still Mom and I'm just glad she got to come and didn't cause any drama. I know your relationship with her is complicated, but I hope it's okay that she's here. I guess this new guy has a lot of money."

"It's your day," I say. "And that's what I've heard."

"At least she can't get drunk and hit on every single man above the age of eighteen here since she's already got a boyfriend."

I roll my eyes a bit. Mom has never been a good role model when it came to the men she dated or how she was constantly flirting with guys. "True."

Noah gives me a hug. "I'm happy for you sis, if Sam makes you happy, then I'm happy."

"He does."

"Good."

We walk back to the wedding party, where Sam and Tally are waiting for us.

"I'm sorry about how I reacted," Noah tells Sam. "I'm a little surprised still, but I am happy for you."

"Thanks, man." Sam gives Noah a hug. "Now go hang out with your wife."

Noah grins at Tally as they make their way to the small cafe where we'll be eating dinner soon.

"You good?"

I smile up at Sam. "Better than good."

37

SAM

"Dance with me." It comes out like a command, which is not what I meant, I don't want to tell Annie what she has to do; she has too much history with men like that. But my heart stops when she looks up at me. She's got a sly sort of grin on her face.

We just finished the wedding dinner and everyone else is talking amongst each other, but I want to dance with my wife.

"Bossy Sam? I like it." Annie takes my hand and I pull her up from her seat. Watching as the soft cotton of her dress falls around her. She's like a dream.

"You like when I'm bossy?"

She nods as she follows me onto an open patch of grass. "Yes, surprisingly. Probably because it's so different from normal Sam and YouTube Sam. But I like every version of you."

"Which is your favorite?" The question is like a lit match, about to start a fire, but I have to know.

She smiles up at me as she wraps her arms around my neck. "I think I'll keep that to myself for now."

I squeeze her hips. "No fair."

"I've got to keep some things a secret. But I will let you know when I like something, deal?"

"Deal." Because what else am I supposed to say? Annie is too good for me, and I'm terrified she's going to wake up and realize that any second and then she'll bolt. I've been right in front of her for years, and she didn't notice me romantically until this past year, so what does that mean for the future?

She lays her head on my chest, and I'm thrown back to last night, with her in my arms. Where I want her to stay forever.

"Is it weird to you that we now have one more night at the same resort where your brother is staying for his honeymoon?"

She shudders against me. "I did not need that reminder or image in my head."

I chuckle. "Sorry, sunshine."

"You are not sorry." Annie hits my chest playfully.

"What should we do tonight?" I ask her.

"Sleep, like last night," Annie says and relief fills my chest. She wants me to be with her.

"I love that plan," I tell her. I'll hold onto this feeling for as long as she'll let me.

Noah wasn't wrong when he voiced his concerns about me not ever having a long term relationship, but he didn't know that the only reason those relationships didn't stick was because I've always been in love with Annie and no other woman was her. No other woman can ever compare.

We dance on a patch of grass, close to the reserved section of the small beachside restaurant where the reception was held. There's a man singing and a crowd has gathered, but the grass patch is empty.

"No one else is dancing, Sam," Annie says, but she's smiling.

"So? Is it so wrong to want to dance with my wife?" I pull her into my arms as the man starts to sing a song by Queen.

Annie throws her head back in a laugh, and my heart lifts. After so many months of seeing her so guarded, it's so nice to see her so carefree. "Are you going to call me your wife forever?"

I rest my cheek against her forehead. "Yeah, I think I will."

"I like it," she says as we sway together in time. "But it'll take some getting used too."

"Mhm," I murmur in agreement. As we dance, I notice a man glued to the baseball game that's playing on one of the TVs at the bar in the restaurant, and the humid, salty air assaults my senses, but I love it. I know that every time I'm near the ocean, I'll remember this moment.

I know that going to Colorado is going to change things, that here at this resort, everything feels magical and even more romantic. But I'm ready to show Annie all the love I've been holding in for years. I know she'll try to pull away, try to do things on her own and not let me in, but I'm going to be there for her every single time. I can't imagine a life without her—I don't want a life without her. And I'll take every moment I can to show her that I mean that.

I hear her yawn. "Should we get you to bed? We've got a long day tomorrow."

By some miracle, we're both on the same flight home, even though Annie had no clue I was living in Colorado. But I upgraded my seat so that I could sit by her. She doesn't have to fly alone, ever again if I can help it.

"Yes, please," Annie yawns again.

I'm driving to us her little cabin that's on Hannah's property. Since I parked my car at the airport we didn't have to get an Uber. I keep glancing at Annie, and I know something is off.

Her walls are going up. I see it happening in real time the closer we get to Estes Park. When it happened on the plane and she got all quiet and less touchy, I chalked it up to flight anxiety. But she hasn't changed since we've landed. She avoided meeting my eyes as we waited for our luggage and that's when I knew. She's getting ready to block me out again.

"You'll love it," Annie is telling me. "The cabin is gorgeous and looks out to the prettiest view of the mountains. And I can't wait to show you the cafe, it's going to be so great. We can go there tomorrow, since I think we're both too tired tonight."

It's eight in the morning and I'm exhausted from traveling all night. I keep telling myself that Annie is only getting quieter and less touchy because she's so tired, but I'm afraid she's putting up her walls.

She's figuring out how to let me down easy, because she's afraid. But I'm not going to let that happen. She doesn't get to do that, not again. Not when I've seen how happy we are together, not when I know that she completes me.

The cabin is dark when we arrive—the curtains all drawn, but it's cozy, just like Annie said it would be.

"Annie—" I start but she cuts me off, still not looking at me.

"I'm really tired, Sam, can we talk after we get some sleep?"

"Sure, sunshine," I say, worry filling my gut. Later, I'll tell her just exactly what I feel for her and that I'm not gonna let her walk away from our marriage, unless that's truly what she wants to do—and not just because she's scared.

38

ANNIE

Sam is still asleep when I sneak out of the cabin. I walk the half mile to Hannah and Graham's cabin and knock softly on the door.

Hannah opens a minute later, two steaming mugs of hot chocolate in her hands. Because just like Tally, my brother's new wife, my dear friend loves hot chocolate more than just about anything. I texted her yesterday, telling her I needed her this morning and she told me she'd be up and ready. Because Sam and I woke up around dinner-time yesterday, made some Top Ramen (not my favorite thing, but it's what I had) and went promptly back to bed.

"Is Graham up?" I ask and she shakes her head.

"No, he's getting some good sleep so we can plan our next hiking trip in a month. We've got a group of four that are coming and he's thrilled, but he wants to rest as much as possible before we spend a few days in the mountains with a bunch of people in their early twenties."

"Aren't you still doing camp?" I ask her, surprised. She and her husband have been running a camp for people who struggle with different mental illnesses every summer. She's been getting ready for it the whole time I've been here. I would have remembered if she mentioned hiking."

"We are, but Graham wanted to try out these hiking expeditions this year and I thought it would be fun. Camp starts next week and will run all of July, then in August we'll be hiking."

I take a sip of my hot chocolate. "Cool."

"But I know that's not the real reason you needed to come over here. Tell me everything."

"I kissed him," I tell Hannah. "A lot, we've kissed a lot. And we slept in the same bed every night."

She squeals, just like I knew she would. Her love story with her and Graham was a windy road, but they got their happy ending in the end and I guess the same goes for me and Sam.

"You slept with him? Go Annie! Emily will be so proud."

I flush. "No, not like that. We just *slept* in the same bed. I'm not ready for anything else yet...I want to go slow."

"I really need to meet this man," Hannah smiles at me. "Because I don't believe you. I think you are ready, but that you're just scared."

I shift uncomfortably. She's not wrong, but I don't want to admit it.

"Well, I'm sure you'll meet him soon, he's asleep in my cabin right now."

"What?" Hannah jumps up. "And you left him to be here with me? Now I know you're freaked. You're trying to run. Again."

I sigh. "It's not that simple, Hannah."

"Sure it is." She looks at me. "You love him, right?"

Tears well up in my eyes. "More than anything, I just hate that it took me so long to realize it. And I don't think I can do this to him. My nightmares, the panic attacks, it's a lot for me to deal with, I can't put all of that on him and expect him to deal with it too. He should be with someone who's carefree and doesn't have all these issues."

Hannah snorts. "Everyone has issues, Annie. And if Sam is half the man you've made him out to be, then I don't think he's going anywhere. Sure, it'll be hard. Living with a mental illness is tough on a couple for sure, but you can do it."

"I don't deserve his love," I say quietly, voicing the fear that's been swirling in my head ever since we left Hawaii. "He's too good, and I don't deserve that."

She sets down her hot chocolate mug and looks out at her land, "I used to think that too."

"What?" I gasp, it's hard for me to believe that she ever felt the way I do. I know she's struggled with depression her whole life, but she and Graham are so in love.

Hannah nods and looks at me. "I haven't told you this part of my story, even though you know so much of the hard stuff. But I left Graham for a while, I broke off our engagement and a few other things happened, but I didn't think I was worthy of his love. And I'd told myself that so much that I believed it and I tried to convince Graham of that. It became too much for him, he got tired of trying to show me the truth—that he was always going to love me—and I could see that, so I left."

"But you're so worthy of love. Everyone is," I tell her.

Hannah nods and gives me a smile. "Everyone includes you. And I'm not going to tell you how to live your life, but if you really love him—and I think you do—you need to tell him and you need to work through the thoughts that he's too good for you and that you're not worthy of his or anyone's love, because you are."

I'm quiet. Logically, her words make sense to me. But after Mitch, it's been hard for me to feel worthy of any kind of love. I never had a mother who genuinely cared about me and I probably never will. But I don't have to keep her in my life, it's okay to cut that tie because all she's ever been is critical and mean.

I don't feel worthy of Sam's love because of my own mental health, because of all the years I spent telling him that I never wanted to date, but he stuck around anyway. I spent most of the day yesterday regretting that we spent so much time kissing while we were in Hawaii. I feel like I'm not ready to go full speed, even if I want to. My mind doesn't feel ready. I can see so clearly how much he loves me and I don't want to hurt him by not loving him the same way, even though I feel that love in my heart.

"Just think about it," Hannah says. "And go back to him, I'm sure he's going to be less than thrilled if he wakes up without you."

"Yeah?"

"You're freaking amazing, my best friend in the entire world. He'd be sad if you aren't there, worried even. You carry all of your emotions right on your sleeve. I bet he knows all of the thoughts you've been having without him having to hear them. Go to him."

I nod, setting down my hot chocolate. "Thanks for the drink, want to do lunch tomorrow? Or sometime before you leave me to go into the wilderness?"

Hannah laughs. "I'm not leaving you. I'll be back in two weeks, and you could come if you want."

"Hiking is not my thing," I say, laughing back.

"I know, but someday, I'll get you to come with me."

"You'd be the only one who could," I tell her truthfully.

"I know." She smiles at me. "Now go tell your man you love him."

39

SAM

I pace back and forth across the creaky floor in the wood cabin again. I already tried calling Annie, but her phone rang on her nightstand.

"Where did she go?" I whisper. I don't know anyone here, I don't know how to get ahold of Annie's friend Hannah, though I know this cabin is on her property, but I don't know how to find Annie.

The door swings open and the morning light falls into the cabin and I rush to Annie, pulling her into my arms.

"You left," I say, emotion filling my voice.

"I'm sorry," she answers, hugging me back. "I needed to talk to Hannah about something."

"And you couldn't have left a note? Woke me up and told me that you were going?" I ask. I know I sound frantic, possessive even, but I can't help it. I was afraid she'd left me again, for good. After she was acting last night, I have no idea where we stand.

She looks up at me. "I had to work through some things."

I swallow. This is it, this is where she tells me that she's done, that she can't be with me because she's too afraid and doesn't want to take the risk. But I'm not going to let that happen. "Wait, before you say anything, I have something to say."

She blinks, but doesn't stop me.

"I love you, Annie, more than anything in the entire world. I need you like I need oxygen. For years, I told myself that simply being your friend was better than nothing, and it was, for a time. But now I need you. I love you. I want you. You are my *wife*. I want to have a real marriage with you. A house with a wrap-around porch, kids if you want them, and to grow old together. We'll be eighty-seven and eighty-nine and I'll still be so in love with you."

"I know you're scared, terrified even. I don't know what the future will hold but I can promise you this, that even if we fight, I'll come back to you. Even if we drive each other crazy, I'll still love you and take you to bed at night and show you just how much I love you. I'll spend every single day for the rest of my life loving you and showing you just how much you mean to me."

When I look at Annie, her eyes are swimming with tears.

"Are you finished?" she asks me, quietly and my heart sinks.

I nod, slowly.

She reaches up and touches my face, moving it so I'm looking at her. Better take this break up like a man, even if it will break me completely.

"I love you, Sam," she says and I let out half a sob.

"You love me?" I ask. She reaches up and wipes away a tear.

"I love you so much. I'm so incredibly, stupidly in love with you. And I fought it for so long. I was so afraid, afraid to ruin our friendship, afraid that I'd end up like my mom. Afraid that I'm too hard to love because too many people have told me that I am."

I cradle her face in my hands. "Loving you has been the easiest thing I've ever done."

Annie grins up at me. "I love you. And I want all the things you want. A house, a family, us growing old together."

I press a kiss against her smile. "I love you, sunshine."

"I love you too," I tell him and kiss him back. He moves us slowly toward the bed, shutting the door behind us and easing me down against the sheets.

"I want to kiss every inch of you, every single freckle. I want all of them," he says reverently as he looks at me, watching my face. "I also can't wait to kiss your tattoo. You got it for me, all those years ago, because of the ring."

I nod. "I want every part of me to be yours," I tell him and I feel the fear slide away as he watches me and leans forward, pressing a kiss on each of my cheeks before moving to my neck and leaving a trail of kisses there.

"You've always been mine, sunshine." I push my fingers into his air and let out a gasp as he nips at my collar bone. "I can't tell you how happy I am that you finally realized it."

EPILOGUE
ANNIE

One Year Later

"You ready for this, sunshine?" Sam grins down at me as I take one last look around our new cafe, *The Wednesday Cafe*. Sam came up with the name, a not so subtle nod (if you're a Swiftie) to Taylor Swift's song "Begin Again". It happened not long after we got to Colorado, when I told him that that song made me think of our love story. I feel like it's perfect.

Today is the opening day. I glance around the cafe. The shiny white tables and my new staff all smiling at me. This is the last moment where the cafe is still just ours.

"I'm ready." I smile at Margot, my last hire and new sous chef. She grins back at me.

"Let's open the doors, then." Sam grabs the giant scissors he bought for the ribbon cutting ceremony. We step outside and it's as if the entire town has gathered for the opening of our new brunch cafe. Which, if I'm being honest, it probably is most of the town.

He offers me the scissors but I shake my head. "Let's do it together."

Together, we cut the ribbon and cameras flash and people cheer.

"I'm so proud of you, sis," Noah says, appearing out of nowhere and giving me a hug.

"I still can't believe you came," I say looking between him and Tally who's six months pregnant.

"And miss the grand opening of your first place? No way," Noah tells me. "But, can we eat first? Because Tally's getting hungry."

"I am eating for two you know," she says but she smiles up at him and it takes everything in me to not put my hand on my own stomach. I found out three days ago that Sam and I will be parents in eight months. I haven't told him yet. I'm planning to tell him when we go to Hawaii in a few weeks. Just like he promised, we're going again, and this time we're going to renew our vows and have a real ceremony, right on the beach. Just the two of us, again. Emily wasn't thrilled when I told her that part. But I did promise her she could throw us a proper party once we get back.

I've got a tiny little onesie in my Amazon shopping cart to bring along to tell Sam that he's going to be a dad. I thought I'd be more nervous about the idea of becoming a mom, but going through this parenting journey with Sam? That makes me feel like I can do anything. He makes me feel like I can do absolutely anything.

This past year has been the best of my entire life. My anxiety isn't gone and I still have PTSD episodes, but things are a lot better than they were thanks to therapy, medication, and Sam's love. He can't fix my brain, but he loves me anyway and I'm grateful everyday for it.

I haven't been back to New York, not since I left, and I'm okay with that. I didn't end up testifying about Mitch, but I didn't end up needing to. The defense had enough with a few other women who came forward with their own stories. He's a real piece of work, and he'll spend the rest of his life paying for what he did. I'm finally at peace, knowing that part of my life is in the past and I won't ever have to see him again.

I take a deep breath, looking at the crowd who came to celebrate the opening of my cafe. I can't believe this moment is real.

"Shall we?" Sam gestures to the cafe and I lead the way inside and he follows me into the kitchen.

The hum of the machine comes to life as the first ticket—probably Noah and Tally's—comes through. "Here we go, people."

I smile as I start the breakfast sandwich on the order. My life didn't turn out the way I expected it to, it turned out even better. My life is so beautiful and I'm so grateful I got a chance to begin again.

"Order up!" I ring the bell and one of the servers grabs the food, before I can start on the next order, Sam pulls me to him.

"Congrats, sunshine," he says and then he kisses me. "I think we'll need to celebrate tonight."

"We will indeed," I say. "Any ideas?"

"I've got a couple." Sam's eyes are twinkling as he smiles and me and butterflies swirl in my belly. It's a feeling I expected to disappear after a few months after we passed the honeymoon stage of our relationship, but this man never fails to make me go weak at the knees.

"I can't wait."

"I love you, sunshine."

THE END

ACKNOWLEDGMENTS

Here we are again, and honestly, I feel more gratitude and awe every time I get to write this section of a book.

I am so so grateful to my family, specifically Griffin and Von. Thank you for loving me and living with me as I try to do this author thing. You're both the best.

Thank you to Marie Soleil and McKenna for beta reading this one. You both helped make this book better. Thank you to Kristen Hamilton, who is an awesome editor! Thank you for making this book what it is.

Thank you to Taylor Swift who will probably never read this, but your music has gotten me through pretty much every life event. I've found so much healing through your words, which is why I had to make Annie a Swiftie. I decided officially to write the book the morning you announced Red (Taylor's Version). It felt like a sign that afternoon when I logged online and saw that you'd shared your re-record was coming. Thank you for making music. Okay, I'm stopping now because I could make this longer.

Thank you to my parents and my extended family who are so so so supportive and always wanting to read my books and share them with people. I love you all so much.

And I wanted to leave a quick thank you to the friends and family who stood by my side many years ago when I was trapped in an abusive relationship. Thank you to my parents, McKenna, Racquel, Bronte, Spencer, Jared, Josue, and Bradley who believed me and stood by me. Thank you a million times over.

I also want to thank God, who I feel has been with me throughout this whole process.

And last, but certainly not least, thank YOU, dear reader, for picking up this book and giving me a chance. I am so so grateful to you for reading my words. I hope they brought you some joy. I wouldn't be here if it weren't for you.

ABOUT THE AUTHOR

Taylor Epperson has dreamed of writing books since she was a kid. She firmly believes that every story needs kissing and romance. Her stories will make you swoon, laugh, and maybe cry. But hopefully, they'll always leave you feeling a little happier.

When she's not writing, you can find her curled up with a good book and a bag of potato chips or playing with her daughter. She enjoys binge-watching cooking shows and crime dramas. She lives in Northern Colorado with her husband, daughter, and very anxious black lab.

ALSO BY TAYLOR EPPERSON

The Nelson Sisters Series

The Luck of Finding You (Tally + Noah)

The Rules of Mistletoe (Holly + Drew)

Begin Again (Annie + Sam)

Sunkissed Summer Novella

Off Trail Love (July 2024)